COYOTE HOME

COYOTE HUNGER BOOK 1

RHIAN CAHILL

RHIAN CAHILL

Coyote Home
Coyote Hunger Book 1
By Rhian Cahill

For more information visit:
www.rhiancahill.com

For the man who rocks my world. Together forever.

1

RUN

THE THUMP of paws hitting hard ground echoed off the valley walls, twigs snapped and leaves were crushed in the mad dash through the forest. Adrenaline pumped through veins pounding with the exhilaration of running free. Rowan loved to run in coyote form but tonight wasn't any old frolic in the woods. Tonight was about escape.

Quinn raced beside her, his beating heart and heavy breaths a welcome comfort. They ran together, darting between trees and through the underbrush as they made their way over the mountains. Speed was important. Quinn needed to be back in Whispering Springs before morning or questions would be asked too soon. Rowan needed to be far from home before anyone discovered her missing.

Her injuries from Marcus' attack were quickly repairing but she still felt dull aches rippling through her muscles. She leapt over a fallen log and the pack strapped to her back shifted to the side, throwing her off balance. Rowan stumbled, her front paws losing their grip in the slippery debris of rotting leaves littering the forest floor. The ground rushed up to meet her and pain exploded in her head. With a yelp, she crumpled to the dirt.

"Rowan!"

Quinn had shifted back to human form and was on his knees beside her, the strap of his pack digging into his bare chest. He ran his hands along her fur-covered limbs, her side and over her skull. His fingers gently probed for any injury. Rowan panted for breath and waited for the dizziness to fade before she changed from coyote to human.

"I'm okay," she gasped. "Just winded."

He reached for the snap on her pack and flicked it open. The tightness in Rowan's chest eased slightly and she drew in a deeper breath as the bag fell to the ground behind her.

"Thanks."

"We'll rest here for a bit." Quinn removed his own pack and placed it beside them.

Rowan pushed off the ground and sat cross-legged, her uncovered ass connecting with the cold floor. Her body protested the move but she didn't have the luxury of being a wimp tonight or ever again for that matter. She dragged her bag closer, unzipped it and pulled out a water bottle. With a flick of her wrist, she popped the top and took a couple of gulps before handing it to Quinn.

His hand wrapped around hers but he didn't take the container. Rowan looked up to find him staring at her. The naked longing swirling in his gaze heated her blood and called to her coyote. Already close to the surface, her beast answered with a call of her own. Need and want zapped through her. Quinn's hand shook, the fine tremors vibrating along her skin in an electric wave that made every instinct she had scream with desire.

He squeezed her fingers before he removed his hand with a growl. "Damn, I want you."

Rowan watched the struggle he waged inside, every emotion crossed his face as he fought to gain control. She knew Quinn was trying to hold back for her benefit but she didn't need his protection. She needed him.

Before she could second-guess the move, Rowan crossed the distance between them. She wrapped her arms around Quinn's neck and slammed her mouth to his. Her tongue slipped out to trace the seam of his lips. For what seemed like hours he remained motionless, unresponsive to her demanding kiss. On the verge of pulling back, Rowan found herself toppling forward instead.

Quinn fell back, his arms clamped around her waist to hold her close as he took them to the forest floor. He took control, his mouth eating at hers with need and desperation. Rowan could feel the raw emotions rolling off him, or maybe they were hers bouncing back. Tonight might be the only night they'd ever share and she intended to make the most of it.

Years of waiting collided with fear of what was to come and drove them both quickly to the edge. Her nipples pebbled, poked into the hard muscle of Quinn's chest, the contact taking the hunger deeper. Undone by the arousal swamping her, Rowan rocked her hips and rubbed her pussy on the hard length pressing against her. He sucked her tongue into his mouth as his hips thrust up.

His cock slid along her slick folds, bumping her clit and delivering sparks of fire into her core. Her womb clenched and moisture flowed from her body to coat them both. The scent of her cream surrounded them and Rowan's body rippled with the orgasm just out of reach. She tore her mouth from his, gasped for breath as she braced her hands on his shoulders and pushed up.

"Not here. Not like this."

Quinn's plea went unheeded as Rowan sought the one

thing that would calm the frenzy taking her over. She had to have him inside her. Take him until they were one. Her hand slipped between them and her fingers encircled his erection. She squeezed his flesh, stroked him from root to tip. Using her legs, she rose up and guided the head to her opening.

"Rowan."

Their gazes met and as she lowered her body they held their breath. Resistance to the invasion clenched her muscles and sent fear trickling through her.

"You're not ready."

Rowan threw her head back and laughed. The idea that she wasn't ready for this moment was ludicrous when she'd waited the last five years for this very minute. She leaned forward, brushed her lips on his and whispered, "I'm more ready than I've ever been."

She pushed down and a little more of his cock breached her resisting body. The pain was minimal and no doubt would get worse before the sheer pleasure of being with Quinn surpassed it. With small gyrations, Rowan slowly took him deeper. Each inch stretched her walls to the point of pain but not enough for her to stop.

"Jeez, you're killing me here," he ground out through clenched teeth.

Quinn's face and chest were coated in sweat, his muscles straining as he held still beneath her. With one final lunge she buried his length to the hilt. Any pain was quickly gone as sensations she'd never experienced registered. The fullness of having him inside, the way his cock brushed her tender walls, the cradle of his hips supporting hers, all unfamiliar but so right.

A moan slipped from her throat, mixed with the pleasure of being joined to Quinn and the vagueness of when they would be together again after tonight, and rumbled with a ragged edge. She slumped forward, laid her cheek on his chest and absorbed the truth of them together. Now.

"Take your time." His hand caressed her hair, his fingers combing through the strands. "We can stop if it hurts."

Rowan smiled. Quinn always thought of her first. Sadness flooded her as the certainty of being without him in the future clutched her heart. She took a deep breath. Determination to not allow Marcus or his father to take this beautiful moment from them straightened her spine and gave her the courage to take what joy she could from the darkness that surrounded them.

His hand stroked down her spine, a tender touch meant to soothe, not inflame. But when it came to Quinn everything he did had her body on hyper-alert. A shiver trailed his fingers, the gentle shudder not stopping until it reached her curling toes. Heat spiraled in her belly and dripped lower. Her pussy clenched and his shaft pulsed as her walls gripped him tighter.

As her body adjusted to being joined with Quinn the world disappeared. Her mind focused on the pleasure streaking its way toward a peak she'd never reached before. Bombarded, Rowan knew only one thing. Move. She had to move.

"Rowan, do you want to stop?"

Quinn's words came the second she put action to thought. He growled when she swiveled her hips and he slid out until only the head of his cock remained inside her. They both moaned as she reversed the motion. Experimenting, Rowan arched her back and cantered her pelvis. The angle changed and more of her tender flesh burst into flame at the new contact. Her clit throbbed, her sheath quivered and more cream lubricated her swollen folds.

"God, that feels good."

Rowan had to agree. A smile curled her lips and she pushed back to sit, straddling him. Quinn's hands grasped her waist, helped her lift and drop as she found a rhythm that excited them both.

"Damn." His fingers tightened, dug into her sides. "I'm not gonna last long."

Good. She wouldn't be far behind him if she didn't go over the edge first. They'd always stopped before either of them reached the point of no return. An orgasm would mark them and they couldn't afford to risk it until they were ready to be mated and before now that wasn't an option.

She rocked her hips, drove down hard and pulled back slow. Her clit grazed the base of his shaft on every plunge. Muscles coiled, her walls sucking at his length with each pass. Quinn's hand left her side and delved between her legs. His fingers zeroed in on the tight bundle of nerves. Pleasure sharpened and Rowan's movements turned frantic.

Quinn finally moved under her. He'd given her control until now but he took it from her with lightning speed. He thrust up, driving his cock impossibly deep. His hands splayed on her hips and he held her still while he fucked her. She rode the razor edge of her orgasm, almost, but not quite going over. A growl filled the air and Rowan's world tilted.

He spun them, had her on her hands and knees before her next heartbeat. Her fingers curled into the dirt and leaves as Quinn's thighs met hers. His hot length probed between her legs and with one hard thrust he sank back inside her welcoming pussy. Rowan's back arched and she pushed her ass against him, taking him deeper. Quinn curled his front over her, their hot, slick skin sliding together.

The slap and squelch of flesh meeting flesh filled the air, mixed with the scent of sex and teased and tantalized until Rowan's breath became jagged rasps of fire lancing her lungs. His fingers found her clit, he circled the wet bud, pinched it—tugged. Sensation splintered and stars flashed before her eyes.

Her womb clenched, her pussy clamping around the hot rod impaled in her depths.

A scream ripped from her throat as her orgasm tore through her. Quinn continued to pound into her from behind, his hands gripping her waist to hold her still. Her head and shoulders dropped to the ground, leaves mashed into the side of her face but nothing mattered but the delirious bliss rolling over her.

The growl that rumbled in the air made her jump, the snarl quickly followed by a howl made her coyote lie down and open for her mate completely. Quinn's chest connected with her back and Rowan raised herself up and arched into him. She turned and dropped her head, offered him the tender slope of her neck to sink his teeth into.

Sharp canines scraped her skin, the sting more tingle than pain. Quinn's fingers continued to strum her clit. Her orgasm had receded only to be driven back up again by his caress. He growled against her neck, the sound vibrating down her spine and into the heat simmering in her belly. His thrusts turned into erratic, frenzied pumps of his cock into her convulsing pussy.

Quinn jerked and buried himself to the hilt. Hot spurts of cum bathed her cervix as he sank his teeth into the side of her throat. There was no pain, a slight sting before fiery tingles raced out in a game of chase. Ribbons of delight connected erogenous zones and pulled tight. Spasms started low and deep, spiraling out until they dropped her off the edge again.

Spent, they slumped forward, crumpling to the floor in a tangled mess of bodies and limbs. Quinn rolled to his side and took her with him. He cradled her in his arms, his ragged breath bathing her neck and shoulder. Rowan's breathing was just as harsh, as was the pounding of her heart against her ribs. Her bones felt as solid as cooked noodles and Rowan wondered if she'd ever be able to walk again.

Reality started to return with the night sounds of the forest around them. She knew they had to get up and keep going. If they were going to make the rendezvous site and give Quinn plenty of time to get back to Whispering Creek before daybreak they needed to go now.

Rowan turned in his embrace. "We need to go."

"A minute more won't hurt." He dropped a kiss on her nose. "Rest for a second and then we'll head out again."

By the time their bodies cooled they'd regained their breath. Rowan was the first to move, Quinn gave her one last squeeze before letting go. Neither spoke as they retrieved their bags. Rowan stashed the water bottle inside before stretching the elastic strap and locking the clip into place. The band pinched but once she shifted to coyote form it would be a perfect fit.

"Ready?"

"No, but do we have a choice?" Quinn asked.

Rowan didn't answer him. They both knew this was their only option now that Marcus had attacked her. With the senior Connelly as sovereign, Quinn and Brogan had no way of protecting her against Marcus' advances. No matter how violent he'd become, his father refused to stop him. And with Connelly's supporters firmly in place, Rowan's only hope was to leave and return when it was safe.

The question was, how long would it take to rid the pack of the evil that had taken hold after her and Brogan's parents had died?

2

QUINN SLOWED, turned to sniff the air and waited for Rowan to catch up. They'd taken the last thirty minutes at a walk, the steep descent needed concentration and careful steps. Even in their coyote forms, this ridge was treacherous. She caught up and stopped beside him, her head tilted to the side, she waited for his lead. He wanted her again. Once wasn't enough and before dawn she'd be gone.

They were less than fifty feet from the valley floor and he knew of a small secluded section of rock face that almost formed a cave. He'd head there and they could take a break before moving on. Quinn was satisfied the only other person in this area of the mountains was Brogan and he, about an hour behind, was trailing them at a discreet distance. Rowan didn't know her brother followed, it was just a precaution but they couldn't risk going without him.

He nodded for her to follow and made his way down the last few feet of mountainside. There had been plenty of time to think after their mad dash through the forest. Once they'd cleared the second ridge the chance of anyone seeing them had been unlikely. Only a few pack members lived beyond the town center and those that did chose the eastern side, not the west.

Getting Rowan off the mountains and away from Marcus quickly and with as much stealth as possible meant their best bet was going west. It had taken less than ten minutes to make their plan and put it into action. It had taken twice that for Rowan and Brogan to talk him out of going after Marcus the second Rowan had told them what had happened. He stumbled on a loose rock when the image of her bruised and bleeding as she staggered through the back door flashed through his mind.

His animal had come roaring to life, ready to rip apart the threat to his mate. It didn't matter that they hadn't completed their mating. For years they were forced to wait, first Rowan's age and then the death of her parents had stopped them. And since that fateful day no one in the pack made a move without the sovereign's okay and there was no way in the world the current sovereign would okay their joining.

Malcolm Connelly ruled by brute strength and intimidation. The once prosperous pack now floundered under his leadership. Quinn and Brogan were working to improve the stability of the pack but the younger members were leaving in droves, there was nothing here but fear and a nonexistent community. Without the next generation, the pack didn't stand a chance of surviving.

They had a plan, were steadily working toward it but with the assault on Rowan he knew things would only get worse from here on. Neither he nor Brogan could protect her from what both Connellys wanted. Standing and support within the pack was what they needed and didn't have. It was only a matter of time before the violence escalated and Quinn wanted her safe. *Needed* her to be safe. And that meant sending her away.

Quinn moved more quickly, Rowan close behind. Not far now and they could rest again. He'd take every extra second with her he could get. The moon, high in the sky, illuminated the rocky section of the valley they headed toward. Small bushes filled this area of the basin, which meant there wasn't as much cover but his senses told him no one else was around to see as they made their way to the darkness of the outcrop.

He shifted back to human form and quickly checked for any animals—dead or alive. His nose told him there weren't any but he wanted to be sure. With the wall of rocks the ground was clear of rotting vegetation and it didn't look like any creature had made this place home since he'd last been here. Quinn stepped back and motioned for Rowan to go first.

She'd shifted and removed her backpack. His body tightened. The sight of Rowan always jangled his nerves but a naked Rowan could jumble his brain in a nanosecond. He blanked out their trek across the mountain and forgot all about the danger she was in. The only thing on his mind was tackling her to the ground and taking her again. With his hands clenched at his side so he didn't reach for her, Quinn followed Rowan into the dark shelter.

"Are we staying here long?"

Her question startled him but it was her naked body suddenly plastered to the front of him that shocked him speechless. She wove her fingers into his hair and pulled his mouth to hers. His cock sprang to life, hardening between them. Their tongues dueled as they each demanded the other give. Rowan's flavor intoxicated— drove him dizzy with lust. The scent of her arousal mixed with the smell of their earlier lovemaking surrounded them in a lush cocoon.

Quinn's hands slid down the curve of her spine to cup her

ass. He squeezed and lifted her against him. Rowan wrapped her legs around his waist and ground her sex against his hard-on. Slick heat coated his swollen flesh and he flexed his hips, rubbing his length over her clit. She bucked into him and threw her head back with a moan. Her breasts rose up and he leaned forward to suck one pointy peak between his lips.

He pulled the delicate morsel deeper, pushed it to the roof of his mouth before retreating and dragging his teeth lightly over the hard tip. Her back bowed and he almost lost his footing. Quinn regained his balance and bent his knees, taking them to the floor quickly. She straddled his hips, her legs crossed behind him to wrap around his torso like a pair of arms.

Rowan held him tight, her breasts pressed to his face and Quinn wasted no time in letting his lips explore her. He licked, kissed and sucked his way across her smooth skin. His beard stubble would leave red marks but he didn't care, he knew by her little cries of delight he wasn't hurting and he wanted to mark her. Wanted her to remember him after she'd left.

The thought of Rowan leaving clenched his heart. It went against everything claiming a mate should be. His coyote howled at the injustice of losing his mate after finally taking her but Quinn's human side knew the only way to truly protect her was to remove her from danger. Until he and Brogan were able to take a stronger standing in the Whispering Mountains pack Rowan would need to remain hidden. He didn't want to think about how long that could take.

Instead he concentrated on the now, and the hot woman in his arms. Quinn nibbled his way up her chest to the slender column of her throat. He nipped with his teeth until she tilted her head giving him better access to the delicate slope. He laved the shallow dip where her pulse beat frantically. A fine film of sweat covered her skin and he lapped at it as he made his way to her mouth.

When he reached her full lower lip he tugged it with his teeth, urging her to open for him. She complied on a moan and he slipped his tongue out to taste her, just a quick lash to tempt her to come play. He tickled the corners of her mouth before caressing the curve of her smile. Quinn kept his actions slow, teasing them both until it wasn't enough. Their breathing grew harsh, the sound amplified by the cavern walls. Their movements got faster, frantic for just the right friction.

Rowan tore her mouth from his and they both gasped for breath. She rocked her pelvis and his cock slid between her slick folds to rest at her opening. He gripped her hips and thrust into her heat. Sunk to the hilt, her flesh scorched him from tip to root. His sac tightened, her sheath like a hot silk cloth draped around his shaft. She began to ride him, up and down, in a slow slide of rippling muscle that threatened to milk the cum from his balls. He wouldn't last long.

Quinn had spent years imagining getting inside Rowan and the reality far outweighed anything his limited imagination could conjure up. Being his mate she was guaranteed to send his hormones into overload but now that they'd joined he struggled to think past burying himself inside her over and over again. If anything this second time felt better than the first.

Her backside slapped on his thighs on each down stroke, the noise echoing around them. She rode him. Took them both up to the peak as if they hadn't sated themselves an hour ago. Quinn leaned forward and clamped his teeth on her tender flesh where shoulder met neck. His tongue licked at the soft tissue caught between his teeth and he bit a little harder. She moaned and dropped her head, nibbling on him the same way.

The orgasm stole his breath but nothing could steal the coyote instinct to claim what was his. Sharp canines pierced delicate skin with the first blast of cum through his cock. A second spurt coincided with an intense burning at his throat where Rowan bit him but he was too far down the magical path of ecstasy to register what it meant. Rowan's pussy clenched, her convulsing walls pulling every drop of cum from the bottom of his balls.

As his heart rate slowed and his lungs started to fill with life-giving oxygen Quinn's body sent out a protest. Pain radiated from his knees and shins, the hard rocky ground unforgiving on his weight-bearing limbs. Rowan lay limp on his chest, her heavy breathing fanning out over his pecs. She'd slumped in his lap as the final wave of her climax subsided. He needed to move her, get them both cleaned up and comfortable.

How he would do that in a dirt-covered, cave-like grotto he didn't know. They had limited supplies in their packs. Just a few essentials for Rowan to take with her in her flight to safety and their water bottles. She had two sets of clothes but nothing else. Even if time had permitted, she couldn't afford to run with much more than what she had. The one thing she did have plenty of was money.

Quinn and Brogan had given her all the cash they had in the house. Quinn had also asked Dale to get her some more, he'd told his friend he'd replace it once the bank opened on Monday. He wanted more than anything to go with her but if they ever hoped to return the pack to a prosperous one, he and Brogan needed to work together to make it happen. It was up to the younger generation, those that were left, to see to the future stability of Whispering Springs.

Rowan understood what they wanted to do, *needed* to do. She was the first to say the only way for her to stay safe was to leave the pack. With Marcus intent on having Rowan and his father willing to back him in his quest, no one could protect her well enough to keep her alive. And Quinn feared it would come to that. If she didn't bow to Marcus, and she never would, he'd kill her.

As much as it went against every need and want inside him, Quinn would rather Rowan be alive and away from him than the alternative. He'd just have to work extra hard to make the mountains a safe haven once more. Somewhere that she could return, a place she'd want to come back to. He squeezed her closer, soaked in the warmth and smell of her. If he was going to let her go he wanted to burn the memory of her in his arms, the way she smelled and the feel of being joined with her on his soul.

"I love you."

Her words floated on the quiet night, a balm to the heart that was tearing in two inside his chest.

"I know." He kissed the top of her head. "I love you too."

"I don't want to let you go."

Quinn squeezed his eyes tight, the pain in her voice sliced at his gut. "If for one second I thought we could do this another way, we would." He eased away to look in her eyes. "I want you alive, whether it's by my side or a thousand miles away I don't care. I'll do everything I can to make it safe for you to return. I promise."

He brushed his lips over hers, a light touch to seal his promise. Rowan's mouth opened on a sigh and Quinn took advantage and slipped his tongue into the dark warmth beyond. The kiss was easy, a delicate exploration that stole his breath. Unhurried, he took the time to savor, to memorize every taste, every texture. After she left tonight Quinn had no idea how long it would be before he saw her again—had her again, and he'd be damned if she'd leave without him having all of her.

His cock hardened. They remained joined and he bucked his hips to slide against her slick heat. Her pussy fluttered along his length and more blood pumped into his shaft. Rowan groaned into his mouth. The sound echoed through his head and sent his pulse pounding in his ears. She rolled her pelvis, rocked them together in a slow rhythm that drove his arousal higher. Quinn wanted to slam into her, his coyote wanted hard and fast but the man wanted, *needed* soft and slow.

Rowan broke their kiss, trailed her lips down his jaw and continued until she nibbled on his throat. Her hands inched over his shoulders, down his back. When her fingers connected with his pack they both froze. Quinn was stunned to realize he still wore the bag. They both reached to undo the clasp, their hands tangling and making the task difficult. Laughter spilled from Rowan and he soaked in the sound, added it to his store of memories.

"How did we manage to not notice this before?" She nudged his hands away and quickly snapped the clip free.

He smiled. "More important things to notice I guess."

Quinn cupped her breasts, flicked her nipples with his thumbs and Rowan sucked in a breath. Her chest rose and filled his hands with her warm flesh. He leaned forward, drew a taut peak into his mouth and the pack hit the ground behind him. Her fingers curled around his head and held him close. Not wanting to disappoint, he did as her action suggested and sucked harder.

Her nipple puckered hard as a rock against his tongue and Quinn clamped the small bud between his teeth. Rowan's back arched and her breast pulled from his mouth with a small pop. His cock pulsed as her muscles rippled in a wave from root to tip. He groaned. The sound turned into a growl as she rose up and plunged back down. She dug her fingers into his shoulders, her nails biting into his skin.

Together they rocked, thrusting in counterpoint until Quinn's groin burned with the orgasm building. The first spasms of Rowan's climax sent fire shooting up his spine and bursting from his balls. Cum surged up his length and spewed from the tip to bathe her core. Her cry of release bounced off the rock walls, the sound like music in his ears.

She sat in his lap, her head resting on his shoulder and he wrapped his arms around her to hold her closer. Their skin, hot and sticky, clung, binding them together just as their souls now were.

3

ROWAN WAITED, crouched behind a tree, making no sound. She could hear Quinn moving around behind her but nothing else moved. Her sense of smell had never been that good, she got by but in no way did she compare to Quinn. Then again no one compared to him when it came to scenting the air.

They arrived at the designated meeting point about fifteen minutes ahead of time. Quinn wanted to be in place down the road from the lookout parking lot to make sure nobody followed Dale. Rowan didn't think they had anything to worry about. Dale Turner was a big city cop, he knew what he was doing. Dale's skills were the reason Quinn had called him.

A low hum filled the air, growing into a roar as the vehicle moved up the mountain road toward them. Headlights flashed off the trees around her but the car kept going. She heard the brakes squeal and finally silence. Rowan waited. Quinn wouldn't move up to meet Dale until he was sure they were alone so she held still and ignored the numbness in her feet.

She wore jeans, a t-shirt and sweater. Sneakers without socks. Quinn, on the other hand, was barely covered by a pair of shorts. He'd left both bags at her feet and once he gave her the all clear she'd move everything left into one pack to take with her. The money Quinn and Brogan had given her was in her pocket. Rowan hated the idea of carrying so much on her but she couldn't afford to access her bank account if she wanted to remain undiscovered.

Quinn appeared before her, sucking the breath from her lungs. It wasn't just his near naked state that left her breathless. He'd moved without a sound, she'd had no clue he was there until he popped up in front of her eyes.

"It's clear." He reached a hand out to her. "Come on, we'll fix the bags at the truck."

Dale Turner was bigger than she remembered, then again he was only a boy when he'd left Whispering Springs. Now he was every inch a man. Her fingers tightened around Quinn's. She didn't fear Dale so much as leaving Quinn. Her instincts were screaming to hold on and never let go but the rational part of her knew she had to leave. If she didn't it wouldn't just be her life in jeopardy.

Marcus would stop at nothing to get at her and she knew because he'd told her, he'd go after Quinn and Brogan to get his way. To protect her mate and her brother she had to leave and let them do what was necessary to rid their pack of the evil festering inside. Neither of them could do that if they were worried about her. For the first time in her life she would be on her own and Rowan had no doubt the next few weeks would be the hardest she'd ever experienced.

Even harder than the day they buried her parents.

She walked beside Quinn, head held high like she had all the courage in the world. If it wasn't for her shaking insides she might even fool herself into believing it.

. . .

"DALE." Quinn extended his hand to his old friend. "Long time."

Dale grabbed Quinn's hand, his grip strong. "Too long, but then I don't make it a habit of visiting the mountain now that I've got no family left."

"Sorry about your mom."

"Thanks but it was past time. She'd been sick so long it was a blessing for her to find peace."

Quinn turned to Rowan. "You remember Rowan?"

"I'd like to say it's nice to see you again, Rowan, but under the circumstances I don't think it quite fits."

Rowan smiled, but she didn't look happy, more like she was in pain. "No, the circumstances are not the nicest."

He squeezed her hand and tugged her under his arm before turning back to Dale. "Did you do everything I asked?"

"Yeah, it's all sorted. She'll be out of the state before anyone knows she's left the mountains. After that Rowan can decide where she goes."

"Thanks. I owe you."

"No you don't. This is what friends are for."

Rowan had pulled free of his arms and was busy stuffing every-thing into one of the packs. There was a slight tremor in her hands but other than that it could be any normal day. Except it wasn't and getting it over with quickly wouldn't make it hurt any less.

Quinn knew he was dragging this out but he couldn't bring himself to let Rowan go yet. A few more minutes wouldn't matter.

"Are you ready? We need to get on the road." Dale directed his question to Rowan and Quinn felt her stiffen beside him.

"No, but I don't have a choice do I?"

Dale shrugged. "Not if you want to stay alive."

His friend knew all that was going on in the pack, Quinn

had made sure he'd filled him in on enough detail to ensure he understood the danger Rowan was in. He trusted Dale to see to her safety. The man was one of the few he would consider asking for help. Of the other two, one was at this moment heading back to Whispering Creek and the other was in town keeping a close eye on their mutual enemy.

This was it. He had to let her go and hope like mad it wasn't the last time he saw her. Quinn grabbed Rowan's elbow, spun her into his arms and slammed his mouth to hers. His tongue invaded her mouth and conquered any protest she might have. There was no fight, she gave and took in the same breath. They stood there on the moonlit road and devoured each other. The not-so-gentle clearing of a throat brought them back to earth with a jerk.

Dale had turned his back while they kissed. His discreet action proving Quinn's trust was well placed. He could breathe easy knowing Rowan was in good hands. She stepped out of his embrace and took a deep breath before handing him the spare pack.

"I'm ready. Let's go."

With one final look at him she turned and walked away. Quinn clenched his fists, his jaw, every muscle in his body, fought to keep himself in place and not run after her. They were making the right decision. And if it wasn't right he'd move heaven and earth to fix it.

.

ROWAN STARED STRAIGHT AHEAD. She didn't want to look at Quinn. Didn't want to watch him disappear from view as they drove away. Tears dripped down her cheeks and off her chin to land on her hands clasped tightly together in her lap. Dale started the pickup and she couldn't stop herself. Her gaze darted to the side mirror. He stood at the edge of the forest, a solitary figure in the darkness of pre-dawn hours.

Dale put the vehicle in gear and began to drive. The crunch of gravel under heavy tires grew louder as the car picked up speed. The man watching them leave got smaller with every inch they drove. A sob rattled her chest, the sound a desperate cry from a heart splintering in two. Emotions swelled, bubbling up and over as Rowan's coyote howled for the mate she was leaving behind.

Unable to control the urge, she spun in her seat to look through the rear window. Darkness hid his expression but Rowan knew from Quinn's stance that he hurt as much as she did. Her chest ached and her stomach cramped. The pain almost caused her to double over but she wouldn't turn away, wouldn't deny herself this final glimpse of him. As the truck took a bend in the road Quinn was taken from her field of vision and lowering her forehead to the back of the seat Rowan cried for all they were being denied.

The silence in the cab was broken by Dale's deep voice. "I won't tell you everything will work out." He ran his hand over her back but it was little comfort. "I will tell you that I know Quinn and Brogan well enough to know that if anyone can fix what's wrong with the pack it's those two."

Rowan knew he spoke the truth. Each had the determination and strength to get the job done but the two of them together would be a formidable force. She turned around to face forward and put her seat belt on. Her tears had stopped but the pain hadn't. The ache wouldn't go away until she was home. Back in Quinn's arms.

As the drone of tires rolling over tarmac filled the air Rowan used the mundane sound and the miles they traveled to collect herself. She put her love for Quinn and all she'd left behind in a corner of her heart and closed it off. With each new breath she took, she vowed to do all in her power to help them and if that meant living away she would. She'd be as strong as they needed her to be and when she finally returned she'd take her place in the pack and make her mate and brother proud.

QUINN'S PAWS pounded across the damp earth. He drove his body hard, the need to numb his senses overwhelming as he fought against his coyote to keep heading home. The animal wanted to turn around, follow the truck that had taken his mate but Quinn knew to do so would mean denying them any future at all. The sound of an approaching coyote didn't slow him down.

His coat hung limp, weighed down by the sweat pouring from his body as he pushed it to the limit. Brogan joined him, each running to assuage the ache inside them. Quinn wouldn't use his own pain to diminish his friends. They'd both given up a hell of a lot tonight. Before he knew it they were in the trees behind the house. Slowing, he brought himself to a stop at the tree line.

He didn't want to go forward and he couldn't go back. With a shudder that traveled from his head to his tail he took the first step toward his life without Rowan by his side. Brogan stayed back, allowed him to lead them across the field that was their backyard. Quinn would have to thank him for that consideration later. They reached the front porch and he shifted from coyote to human.

Naked as the day he was born, Quinn sat on the cold front step and stared off into the distance. Silently, his best friend joined him. Lost in his own thoughts he didn't acknowledge Brogan's presence. Didn't think he could speak yet even if he had something to say. It was Brogan who broke the quiet.

"We'll bring her home." His words were a vow, one they both shared.

Quinn tried to talk but all that came out was a croak worthy of a frog. He swallowed, cleared his throat and tried again.

"Yes, we will."

"I can live with her not being here as long as she's safe from Marcus."

"She'd be safe if you let me go after him now," Quinn growled.

"You know you can't do that. Connelly would set one of his henchmen on you in a heartbeat, he just needs an excuse. Don't give him one, Quinn."

"How can you sit back and not want to rip Marcus to pieces for what he did to Rowan?"

"I never said I didn't want to." Brogan sighed. "Truth is it took every ounce of control I have to *not* go after him. I'd love nothing more than to kill him with my bare hands but we both know that isn't going to help any of us."

Quinn let out a breath. He knew Brogan was right. They needed to gain support from the pack, needed to prove to the Council the sovereign should be removed from his position. And the only way to do that was to outsmart him. The senior Connelly would be tricky to trip up, he'd spent years cementing his brand of leadership on the pack and no one was willing to go against him.

Violence would probably be involved but it wouldn't be the way they won this fight. They needed the support of as many councilmen as they could get and they needed to stop the younger generation from leaving the mountains too. Without the future to fight for, the older pack members wouldn't see any point in throwing their allegiance behind Brogan.

"You're right. I just need to get past tonight and then I'll be fine." Quinn hoped he spoke the truth. Living without Rowan would not be easy but he would do what he had to so he could secure their future and that of the pack.

Brogan stood and clapped his hand on Quinn's shoulder. "I'm going inside for coffee. Are you coming?"

"No. I think I need to be outside a bit longer. Maybe go for another run." Energy vibrated through his body, his coyote stirring with renewed hunger. He wanted to break free and run. But Quinn was in control. The animal urges would not get the best of him. Standing abruptly, he knocked Brogan's hand off. "I'll be back soon."

He jumped off the steps and without thought he shifted to coyote form and ran. He headed for the ridge that would give him a clear view of his home and remind him of everything he stood to lose if he didn't pull himself together and fight with all he had. As he darted through the underbrush he disturbed creatures just waking from a night of sleep. The forest stirred to life around him, another reminder of all that was at stake.

With speed and agility he made his way up the mountain and to the outcrop that overlooked the house he shared with the Wilder siblings. Pain lanced his chest as he thought of how empty the house would be without Rowan in it. How empty he would be without her.

BROGAN WILDER STOOD at his bedroom window with coffee in hand. He'd known where Quinn was headed, he didn't think his friend should be alone but he gave him the space he seemed to need. He had a clear view of the mountainside and the ridge behind the house. From there, he knew you could see for miles. Raising his mug he took a sip of rich dark liquid.

The sun was almost up and Brogan knew today would be the beginning of a long road. One he wouldn't travel alone but only the toughest would survive it. He wasn't sure how exactly they were going to remove Malcolm Connelly from his position as sovereign but he knew they would. All he had to do was think about what his sister and his best friend were being forced to endure to know he'd do whatever it took to put the pack back to rights.

A small flock of birds burst from the trees near the top of the ridge and Brogan knew Quinn was close to reaching the summit. He understood the need to run, the need to feel in control that was coursing through his friend's veins. Brogan's own blood pumped with the yen to run and never stop but he couldn't afford to give in. Not today and not ever. If he was going to lead the pack into a prosperous future he couldn't give in to the emotion.

His shoulders slumped with all that rested on them. Brogan knew he'd done the right thing sending Rowan away, knew how much easier it would be for them to wrestle control of the pack from Connelly with her safely stashed away. But all the logical arguments in the world couldn't take away the pain of losing his sister. Not even knowing she'd be able to come home one day helped to ease the ache in his heart.

He could only imagine the pain his best friend and sister were suffering. If nothing else he'd make sure both Connellys paid for that. Brogan wasn't a vengeful person but where the Connellys were concerned he'd make an exception. Determination straightened his spine, they would see this through. Satisfied they'd made the right decision, Brogan watched and waited for the new day.

And as dawn broke, a lone coyote stood on Whispering Ridge. In the solitude of the first morning light he threw back his head and howled.

4

HOME

TIMBER CRASHED AGAINST TIMBER. Windows rattled in their frames and the hardwood floor vibrated beneath her bare feet.

Time to face the music.

Rowan turned toward the door. She knew what she would see but knowing and seeing were two different things. Silhouetted by the sun, the six-foot-four wall of solid muscle standing in the doorway was menacing in appearance and attitude. She should be terrified but she'd never been afraid of Quinn. She knew to the depth of her soul that he'd never hurt her no matter what she'd done.

"Hello, Quinn."

"Get your things, you're coming home."

Rowan rolled her eyes. He hadn't changed. Six years hadn't tempered his demanding personality. Then again it had done little to curb her rebellious nature and need to provoke him. In fact, it had increased her need to make her own decisions. Her independence had come at a cost. Being separated from her family, her home—her mate. It had almost cost her sanity.

"No." She wasn't going to allow Quinn or her brother to tell her what to do anymore. She'd finally come home to face her destiny and her mate but she was here on her terms, best to get everyone used to the new Rowan from the start.

"No?" Quinn's brow creased and the confusion swirling in his caramel brown eyes almost made her back down. Almost.

She sucked in a deep breath, stiffened her spine and straightened her shoulders.

"I'm not coming to Whispering Creek yet. I need time."

"Time? For what? And why the hell didn't you tell me you were on an earlier flight?" Anger and hurt simmered in his voice.

"I need to adjust to being home, Quinn."

"You're not home. Your home is Whispering Creek—by my side."

"I am home. Whispering Mountains is home."

"You're not staying here. Get your things or I will."

"No."

"Rowan," he growled.

"Quinn, please try to understand. I've been gone six years—"

"Exactly. You've spent too long away from me already. Get your stuff."

"No. I'm not leaving the cabin until I'm ready."

He took a step toward her, a growl rumbling deep in his bare chest and his eyes flared amber with the anger her disobedience raised. She put up a hand and stood her ground.

"Don't you dare come any closer." To her surprise, he stopped. She swallowed over the lump in her throat. "Please, Quinn. You have to understand. I've ignored my coyote for six years. I can't even remember what she looks like. I need to reconnect, need to be comfortable in both my skins. I can't do that if I have to deal with the pack."

Commotion behind Quinn drew both their gazes. Brogan stood at the door stomping snow and mud from his boots. He stepped into the room and threw a bag at Quinn.

"Get dressed," Brogan barked at Quinn but his eyes were on Rowan. "What the hell do you think you're doing?" he demanded.

Great. Two alpha males to deal with. On their own she knew she could handle them but together, batting for the same cause...

Rowan closed her eyes, tried to focus on what she knew she wanted. What she needed. Dragging in more oxygen, she steeled her determination to get them to see it from her side. The swish of cloth and the metallic hiss of a zipper closing snapped her eyes open.

She breathed easier. Now that Quinn had some clothes on she wouldn't have to deal with the distraction of his naked body. And what a gorgeous body it was, all sculpted muscle and smooth male skin. Memories of exploring his hard male flesh with her hands sent a shiver down her spine. She curled her fingers, clenched them tight to stop her hands from reaching out to touch.

How she hadn't jumped him the second he slammed through the door stark naked was beyond her. There was not one day, one night over the last six years where her body hadn't craved his and all the pleasure tangling with him gave her. She licked her dry lips before speaking to her brother.

"Hello to you too, Brogan."

He looked sheepish for all of two seconds before his face drew into an angry scowl. Rowan sighed. She really didn't want their first meeting to be clouded with anger. But then what she wanted and what she got were rarely the same.

"When did you get in? And why didn't you tell us you were coming early?"

The coffee machine dinged, signaling it was ready. A shot of caffeine was just what this occasion needed. At least she needed it. She turned, reached into the cupboard for two more cups and poured each of them full to the brim. None of them took milk and she'd given up sugar a few years ago.

Quinn moved up beside her, close but not touching. Heat radiated off him and his scent flowed around her, through her. Breathing deeply she pulled him in, filled her lungs with the smell she'd gone so long without.

"Here." He held the sugar bowl out to her.

Raising her gaze to his, she said, "I don't take sugar anymore."

Shock bloomed in his eyes, then confusion.

"It's just one of many things that have changed, Quinn." She tried not to squirm when he leaned in close, sniffed at her neck, her breasts. She knew he was scenting for another male. He wouldn't find one. "That hasn't."

A low rumble was Rowan's only warning. He turned quickly, slanting his mouth over hers. Crushing pressure and his probing tongue had her opening to him. Need slammed into her. Quinn wrapped his arms around her waist, lifting her off the floor and against his body. His hard length trapped between them. Her hands gripped his shoulder, slid into the hair at his nape and over his scalp. She tugged his head closer. Their teeth bumped and scraped and the kiss turned volcanic.

Heat blazed through her blood, pumping into her breasts and pussy, throbbing to a tribal beat only Quinn could drum up. She bent her legs, curled them around his hips and ground her pounding clit on his cock. A snarl vibrated in her chest, her coyote snapped at her control and threatened to break free. Twisting her head, she ripped her mouth from his. It was too much. She felt her grip weaken, knew the beast would spring forward at any second.

"Stop," she panted.

He didn't hear her. His mouth traveled along her jaw and down her neck. Rowan's muscles stretched, her teeth lengthened and her claws popped out and dug into Quinn's scalp.

"Quinn!" Brogan's shout penetrated the hammering in her ears.

Her legs dropped to the floor as Quinn pushed her away to look at her. It was too little too late.

"Fuck!" The word exploded from his mouth.

The animal she'd denied for so long broke free and she shifted before he let her go.

QUINN STARED AT ROWAN.

What the hell just happened?

One minute she was in his arms the next she was shifting. He let go, allowed her to slide to the floor as she changed to coyote. If he wasn't so freaked out he'd laugh at the sight of her in T-shirt and shorts. Brogan made it across the room as Quinn dropped to his knees beside her.

"What the hell happened?" Brogan's words echoed his own thoughts.

"I don't know."

Quinn stroked the fur along her neck. Rowan's eyes drifted closed and she lowered to her belly on a sigh. Her movements were lethargic—listless, as she settled into a comfortable position. A shudder rippled down her canine body and her breathing evened out, slowed, deepened. He knew she'd taken a run earlier, that's how he knew she was here. Brogan had asked him to check on the group of naturals living up on Whispering Ridge—make sure they had a food source. He'd been heading back when he smelled her. Rowan's scent was imprinted on his soul, he'd know it anywhere.

He had run the rest of the way back to the house as fast as his human legs would take him, only to discover she wasn't there. His nose never failed him, he had known she was close. He'd yelled for Brogan to follow, stripped out of his clothes and taken to the forest in coyote form. Excitement and fear in equal measures had swamped him. What was she doing up the mountain? Why hadn't she told him she was arriving today?

Rowan's warmth and scent soaked into him. His fingers tangled in her coat, trailed down her neck and over her side. She whined softly, snuffled and settled back down when he petted her head and murmured soothing words. It didn't matter how she'd gotten here or why she'd come without telling him or Brogan. What mattered was the years of waiting were over.

Rowan was finally home.

"Is she asleep?" Brogan's whispered words were laced with concern.

"Yeah, I think so." Quinn scooped her up in his arms, bundled her against his chest as best he could. Brogan steadied him as he got to his feet. "I'll put her on the sofa, closer to the fire."

"Is she sick?"

"I don't think so. Her temperature feels normal and she talked and looked fine before..." He didn't want to think about the scorching kiss they'd shared before she'd changed in his arms.

He placed her on the sofa and settled on the floor in front of her, continued to stroke her coat, more to soothe himself than Rowan. Brogan brought the cups of coffee she'd poured them. He passed Quinn his before he sat in the chair opposite. They remained silent, each lost in their own thoughts. Neither voiced their concern about Rowan's sudden appearance. Quinn had no idea how long they sat there while she slept, all he knew was he'd finished the coffee long before her eyes opened.

A sigh of relief huffed from his chest and he smiled.

"Shift back, Rowan," he murmured.

She took a long time to change back and Quinn wondered if Brogan's concern about illness had merit. She looked tired. The dark circles under her eyes were a deep purple and sunken into the tender flesh of her face. He ran his fingertips over her cheek, along her jaw, around her neck and into her hair. Leaning forward, he brushed his lips over hers. Quinn pulled back an inch and kept his eyes focused on hers.

"Hey. How do you feel?"

"I'm okay, just need to rest."

"What happened, Rowan?"

"I've ignored my coyote too long. I can't control the shift anymore." She swallowed hard, licked her lips. "And changing drains my strength."

"What do you mean you can't control it?" Quinn asked.

"It just happens. Like just now, my coyote took over and I couldn't hold her back. I couldn't earlier either."

"Here, drink some water." Brogan offered her a glass. "When did this start?"

Quinn helped Rowan sit up and she leaned back into the sofa, squeezed her eyes shut and took a deep trembling breath. Her eyelids lifted and the tears pooling in the brown orbs tore at Quinn's heart like claws. "Today's the first day I've shifted in six years."

ROWAN WATCHED the two most important men in her life absorb her words. Quinn was the first to speak.

"Not once?"

"No. I couldn't afford to give myself away. I've used everything I could to mask my scent and done whatever it took to go unnoticed."

"Not even when you were alone?" Brogan asked.

"No. You know shifting releases more of your scent."

"So what you're saying is that you need to learn to control your coyote again, like you did at puberty?" Quinn asked.

"Yes, but in the meantime I don't want anyone in the pack to know I'm unstable. You saw what happened when we kissed. I can't control the urges anymore than I can the coyote." She sighed. "All it took earlier was stepping outside and seeing the forest."

"She wanted to run," Brogan said.

"Yes, she did." Rowan looked at her brother. There were signs of aging but other than a few little wrinkles around his eyes and mouth he hadn't changed much. "I got in last night. Drove up in the dark, and with the jet lag, I didn't take much notice of the mountains around me. I just dragged myself inside and crashed. When I went out this morning to get my bags... well let's say things got a little hairy." She laughed at her own joke. Neither one of them found it amusing.

Quinn pushed to his feet. "You're coming home."

He was back to ordering her around. Well too bad. She knew she needed to stay here, away from everyone and everything that would distract her from reacquainting herself with her wild side. She wouldn't let him or Brogan change her plans. All she needed was a couple of days, maybe a week to get her bearings and then she'd be ready to face the pack and all that coming home meant.

"No. I'm staying here." Pleased with the strength in her voice she stared at Quinn. He'd have to carry her out of here to get his way and she doubted he'd resort to that.

"You can't stay here alone," Brogan said.

She turned to him. "Why not? I've been alone for the last six years, Brogan. A couple more days won't hurt."

"You're not going to budge on this, are you?" Quinn's question drew her gaze back to him.

"No."

"Brogan's right, you can't stay here alone. I'll stay with you."

"You can't," she blurted. "Look what happened before. I need to concentrate on gaining control. How am I supposed to do that if you're here? The slightest touch could set me off."

"I won't touch you."

"Right," she scoffed. "We haven't been able to keep our hands off each other since we were teenagers. I don't see us managing it now."

"I won't touch you until you think you're ready. But I'll be here when you can't control your coyote. I'll make sure nothing happens to you when you shift, Rowan." He bent at the waist, leaned in until their faces were so close his breath fanned over her lips. "And when you think you've got control, I'll push you. I'll touch you until you forget your name, never mind your coyote."

Desire blazed in his eyes and she sucked in a breath as her arousal spiked in response.

"But but..." She struggled to remember what they were arguing over.

"You want to stay here. This is the way we do it. If you don't like it get your things and I'll take you home."

She turned to Brogan, pleaded with him silently to intervene but one look told her she wouldn't be getting any help from him. She didn't need him to voice his opinion but he did anyway.

"Quinn's way or no way, Rowan. I'll tie you up and carry you down the mountain myself if you don't agree."

She blew out a breath and fell back against the soft leather cushion. Alpha males and their demanding ways. At least she knew they ordered her around out of concern and not meanness. Other members of the pack used their size and strength to intimidate, enjoyed the fear they instilled in those they tormented. Even with all their faults and bossy alpha ways, Quinn and Brogan loved her. And she loved them. She'd give in on this, but only because it kept her away from the pack and the one person she hoped never to see again.

5

ROWAN RETREATED TO THE BEDROOM, leaving Quinn and Brogan to talk about pack business and how they'd account for Quinn not being around if anyone questioned where he was. They'd gone out to her rental car to retrieve her bags earlier and she busied herself removing her toiletries and a couple of outfits. The rest she'd send with Brogan when he went back to Whispering Creek.

Home.

So close and yet so far. How many times had she dreamed of this moment? For years her nightmares were filled with never being able to return and now to be this close...

"Hey."

She turned to find Brogan lounging against the door jam. He studied her and she tried not to fidget under his close scrutiny.

"Hey, yourself." She smiled and stepped toward him.

He pushed off the wall and met her halfway. When he opened his arms she leapt into his embrace, soaking up his warmth and the love he'd always given her.

"I missed you so much." Her words were muffled against his neck as she drew in his familiar scent.

"I missed you too, Rowan." He squeezed her tight before putting her back on her feet. "But I wish you'd told us what was going on. You wouldn't have had to face this alone."

"I didn't want you to see me like this." She shrugged a shoulder and turned away. "I want you to see me as the strong independent woman I am and not the needy teenager you had to hide away."

"You may have been a teenager, but you were never needy." His hands skimmed down her arms, comforting in their movements.

"I'm sorry."

"No need for sorry. Are those to go home?" He pointed at her still-packed bags.

"Yes, I don't need much while I'm here. I'm not planning on venturing out before I return home." She followed him when he went to pick up her bags. "Oh, and in the next few days there'll be some more of my stuff arriving. I'd planned to be back by the time everything arrived but I didn't bank on having such a hard time with my coyote."

Brogan stroked a hand over her hair. "It's okay, Rowan. Take all the time you need. There's no rush."

Tears flooded her eyes and she blinked rapidly to stop them from spilling. How had she ever survived without Brogan's unconditional love and support?

"Hey, none of that." He cupped her face and brushed at her tears with his thumbs. "It'll be okay, you're home now."

A sob broke free. Her heart hurt with all she'd missed by not being here. She still believed leaving the pack had been the right decision. They didn't stand a chance against a corrupt sovereign and his equally immoral son. Brogan pulled her to his chest, wrapped her in his warm embrace and held her tight while she cried out all the grief she hadn't allowed herself to feel until now.

QUINN SAT BACK and soaked up the sight of Rowan making dinner. Brogan left earlier, choosing not to eat with them. Quinn knew why. The quicker Rowan was able to get control of her coyote, the quicker she'd be going home. Brogan knew the sooner he let her get on with it, the better. Neither wanted her to suffer and they would gladly take any pain or frustration on her behalf but this was something she had to do on her own. He had no clue how he'd be able to sit back and watch her struggle through it. It had almost done him in when she'd been a teenager and he'd had no idea they were mates then. The next few days were going to be tough. For both of them.

Even now his fists were clenched around his knees in a white-knuckled grip. The urge to go to her and fold her in his arms was razor sharp. He knew she'd cried on Brogan's shoulder. He hadn't needed his friend to tell him. Her eyes were red and puffy from her tears and it cut him up inside that he hadn't been able to stop them from falling. That he hadn't been the one to soothe her when they had. Her emotions bashed against his, tugged and pulled until her pain was his. He should be able to protect his mate from everything.

"You can't do this for me." Rowan's quietly spoken words snapped him from his thoughts. He hadn't realized she'd stopped what she was doing and turned to watch him.

"I know, but it won't stop me from wanting to."

"After dinner I'd like to practice shifting but I'm not sure it's a good idea to get naked in front of you just yet."

He grinned. Yep, if she got naked he'd be all but crawling out of his skin to jump her. Kind of like he was now, even with all her curves hidden beneath her T-shirt and shorts, his body pulsed with the need to possess her.

"You could just wear what you've got on. They were loose on you earlier when you shifted."

She scrunched up her pert nose and thought about his suggestion. "Okay. That'll work for now."

Satisfied, Rowan turned back to her dinner preparations giving him a view that made his mouth water. The shorts might not be tight but they were cut high exposing her long lean legs. His tongue tingled with the need to taste those sculpted calf muscles, toned thighs and the slope of her ass. He didn't even want to think about the dimple above the heart shaped cheeks, or the crease between them.

He stifled a low groan. The ache in his rock-hard cock wasn't going to be taken care of anytime soon. Not unless he wanted to do it himself and he knew jacking off wouldn't begin to slake the lust now that Rowan was back. He'd never been with anyone else. He knew that wasn't normal but he'd always been weary of his coyote genes and by the time he'd been ready to take the step into manhood Rowan had hit puberty and everything had changed.

He remembered being at the lodge the night she'd shifted the first time. Remembered the gut slam of need and knowledge that blindsided him the second she'd stepped through the door. It had taken her months to make a full change, the skill taking time to master for all born coyotes. At the onset of adulthood each of them struggled to connect with their dormant animal. She'd been fourteen. Way too young for him to do anything about them being mates. Brogan had almost gone ballistic on him. No, he had. It was the one and only time they'd fought. Once Quinn had made it clear he would wait for Rowan, his friend had calmed down.

The night of Rowan's attack had changed everything. With

Connelly firmly in control of the pack, they couldn't begin to protect her and getting her out had been the only way to ensure her safety. Sending her out into the world without him was the hardest thing Quinn had ever done. She'd been eager to complete their mating ritual and with the added protection of being mated, Rowan didn't have to worry about the attention of other male coyotes. It had been the only time they'd had sex. Until then they'd settled for a lot of making out.

How they'd managed to stop on any of those occasions was a mystery. The taste and scent of Rowan filled him. He didn't need to remember. It was part of him, mixed with his own essence. They were combined forever in a way no one could ever undo. The sizzle in his veins turned to a boil and his jeans threatened to strangle his dick. The damn things were choking the life out of the erection trying to break free of the unforgiving denim. He needed to get out of them. Now. Good thing they kept a supply of clothes here at the cabin.

His chair scraped over the timber floor as he pushed away from the table. Rowan spun around, eyes wide, legs braced. It shocked him to see her fear. Surely she knew he'd never hurt her.

"I'm just going to get cleaned up and changed." He watched, waited for her muscles to relax. When she took a deep breath and smiled, he said, "I'll be about ten minutes."

"It's okay. Dinner won't be ready for about thirty minutes."

He walked over, brushed his fingers over her cheek. "You know I'd never hurt you, right?"

Her eyes closed and she nodded. "Yes."

"Look at me." He waited for her gaze to meet his. "I love you with everything I am. You are all I am. We'll see this through. Together."

Eyes swimming with tears, she stood on tiptoes and brushed her lips over his. A light caress, nothing worthy of racing hearts or raging hormones, but with Rowan there was never anything else. The fire ignited, scorched him from the inside until he all but melted. Stepping back, he put distance between them. It would be so easy to reach out, pick her up and carry her off to bed. His jaw clenched hard enough to take a layer of enamel off his teeth. He took another step away from temptation and damn if she didn't work out what he was doing.

The Rowan he knew peaked out, sparkled in her eyes and tipped her mouth into a saucy little grin. An answering smile teased his lips.

This is what he wanted to see. His Rowan, not the one who jumped at the slightest noise. The one who teased and laughed and wasn't afraid of him or what he made her feel. And until this moment he hadn't realized how hurt he was by her fear of all they were to each other. That would change. He'd make sure it changed. Before long he'd be able to hold his mate in his arms without either of them worrying about her losing control of her coyote.

"I'll be back," he said in his best Terminator impersonation.

She threw back her head and laughed. A belly deep, care-free gale that fizzed in his blood and brought light to his heart as the echo of it followed him out of the kitchen.

TEN MINUTES in a cold shower and he still had a hard-on to rival the Eiffel Tower. The sweat pants didn't hide it either but there was no way he was putting another pair of jeans on. He wanted to be able to use his cock when Rowan was ready and he risked permanent damage if he stuffed himself into what amounted to a denim torture device. He walked out into the living room, his erection pointing the way.

Rowan was setting the small dining table with plates when

he came up next to her. Her gasp and wide eyes had him covering himself with his hands.

"Sorry. You've always had that effect on me and it's not going to go away until after..." He didn't want to voice what would help the problem. "Just ignore it. I'm going to. Well I'll try at least."

"This isn't going to work. I can't expect you to put up with —" she stalled, waved her hand in the direction of his tented pants. "It's got to hurt."

"See now, the hurt isn't what I'd call pain and if I left I'd be in the same state. I can live with it. It's less than what you'll be going through and I've already told you I'm not going anywhere. We do this together."

She blew out a puff of breath, her bangs fluttering out of her eyes. "Fine. But don't complain when you've got blue balls." Turning, she stomped off into the kitchen to retrieve dinner.

"What can I do to help?" he asked, following her.

"Grab the green salad from the fridge and put it on the table. What do you want to drink? Coffee or soda?"

"I'll grab a soda. What are you having?"

"I'll have one too."

They said nothing more until their plates were full and they'd made inroads into filling empty stomachs. The silence was comfortable and neither felt the need to fill it with mundane chatter. It had always surprised Quinn, their ease with each other. Even before Rowan had hit puberty and they realized they were mates, the relationship between them had been more than her being his best friend's little sister. For as long as he could remember she was a part of him. Long before they'd crossed into physical intimacy, they'd been emotionally intimate.

He'd never balked at telling her anything. She was his past, his present and his future. And he'd see her through this, help anyway he could so she could take her place in the pack and finally come home.

ROWAN LEANED AWAY from the table. She was stuffed so full of food, moving was impossible without rupturing something. Eyes half closed in post pig-out lethargy, she watched Quinn through her lashes. He continued to devour mouthfuls of the stew she'd made. His utter enjoyment was displayed with little moans as he chewed and swallowed every bite. She'd missed his enthusiasm. Nothing was ever done with less than full gusto.

Her gaze followed his hands, the bob of his Adam's apple, the flick of his tongue as it reached out to catch a drop of sauce from the corner of his mouth. She wanted to lean over, slip her tongue out and catch that escaping morsel for him. He was completely absorbed in the task of eating. The meal wasn't anything special, just a basic stew with meat and veggies but he ate it like it was a meal served in a five-star restaurant. Using a piece of crusty bread, he soaked up the last of the gravy, popped it into his mouth and looked up at her.

Smoldering, sated eyes met hers. Bedroom eyes. He'd always had them and they could turn her inside out with a look. Nothing had changed. Her coyote stirred, pulled and pushed to be let free. Rowan held on, stopped the change from happening. She gulped in air, tried to slow her breathing down by closing her eyes and thinking of anything but Quinn. He remained perfectly still, didn't draw a breath and still she felt his presence. Every nerve tingled with desire, need. Muscles stretched, skin pulled and teeth lengthened.

Shudders racked her body and sweat slicked her skin, quickly absorbed by the fur thickening all over her body. It was too hard to hold back and she was too tired to fight her coyote anymore. With a whimper she slid from her chair to the floor and let go.

A chair scraped the floor and then Quinn was next to her, murmuring words of comfort and stroking his fingers through her coat. Her shuddering eased and a sigh escaped her chest. She wanted to sleep. Curl up and sleep, but she couldn't. She needed to muster enough strength to change back. He lifted her head, placed it in his lap while he continued to soothe her with the caress of his hand. It took a few minutes but she didn't drop into oblivion like she had before.

She barked once, pulled away and sat back on her haunches. Her muscles shook, her bones popped, like knuckles being cracked, and then she was human again. She slumped forward, Quinn catching her before she face-planted into the floor. Scooping her up, he rose to his feet as if she weighed nothing and headed for the bedroom.

"Where are you taking me?" she murmured.

"Bed. The circles under your eyes just got darker and after the effort to control and change you just put in I'd say it's time for you to sleep."

"I don't want to sleep. I've got to clean up after dinner."

"Nope. I'll do that. You'll go to bed. I don't care if you just lie there; you're not getting up until morning. I'll take care of the kitchen."

"Quinn." Her protest was weak but she made the effort anyway.

"Rowan," he mimicked her tone.

She smiled as her eyes drifted shut. He laid her on the soft mattress, pulled the quilt up over her and tucked her in as if she were a child. With no energy left to complain, she admitted defeat and snuggled into the comfy bed, her mind sinking into sleep in seconds.

· · ·

QUINN WAITED until her breathing evened out. Sure she'd dropped into a deep sleep, he left the room to tackle the clean up. It didn't take long to cover the leftovers, rinse the plates and stack the dishwasher. He checked to be certain he hadn't missed any dirty plates before filling the powder holder and switching it on, the electrical hum the only noise in the quiet room. He'd locked up earlier but he went around and double-checked the door and all the windows.

He switched off the lights and made his way back to the bedroom. The fact Rowan hadn't mentioned sleeping arrangements told him how exhausted she was. She'd probably go to town on him in the morning but he wasn't sleeping anywhere but next to her from now on. He was never allowing her away from him again.

She was still curled on her side, the quilt tucked up under her chin. Even in the darkened room the shadows under her eyes stood out. He'd make her get plenty of rest. She could practice shifting as much as she wanted but he would do every-thing else. From now on, he'd take care of her, feed her and put some weight on her bones. That had to be part of her problem. She couldn't weigh more than a ten year old. He'd soon fix that. Plenty of food and plenty of rest and he'd be taking her home in no time.

Stripping out of his clothes, he climbed in beside her. For her sake, he left his boxers on but he wouldn't be making any other concessions. He reached over, curled an arm around her waist and snuggled her back against his chest. Her warmth seeped into him. Her scent surrounded him. Her ass fit into the cradle of his hips and his erection pressed into the crease between her soft, squeezable cheeks. It would be so easy to slip inside her in this position.

How they would make it until she gained control was anyone's guess. Holding her while she slept had his heart racing, his groin pounding and his coyote howling to take, to possess. She was his mate, he should be able to have her any way he wanted. Anytime he wanted. He might just end up with those blue balls she predicted earlier. If touching her set off a shift then he'd change as well and there wouldn't be a problem. They'd not mated in their coyote forms and he couldn't deny the thrill the thought delivered.

Quinn smiled into the dark. Maybe they were going about this all wrong. Maybe she needed to connect with her coyote and its base animal needs. She'd held off the change at dinner, he'd watched her struggle before her exhaustion had won out. And then, when she'd shifted back, it hadn't taken as long as earlier in the day. She was already making progress at controlling her coyote.

He pulled her closer, nuzzled the nape of her neck and tasted her skin. She was warm and soft, sliding under his tongue like the sweetest dessert. He shuddered with the need to take what he wanted. To fuck her until they both lay sated. Until they satisfied the mutual cries screaming at them from within.

As much as he wanted to do things her way, Quinn didn't think their coyotes would let them for long. Already he could feel the pull. His beast had its mate within reach and wouldn't be happy to wait. Hell, he wasn't happy to wait but he had to give Rowan her chance. If he didn't she'd fight him and he couldn't risk losing her again. He'd let her go once, there was no way he'd do it a second time.

6

ROWAN CAME AWAKE SLOWLY. Surrounded in warmth, she wanted to stay asleep but something nagged at her mind, made her think she needed to get up now. Stretching, she arched her back and rolled over onto a warm body.

"Ah..." She leapt from the bed, got tangled in the covers and went down on her ass, hard. As pain radiated from her squashed rear end her senses kicked in and a familiar scent filled her nostrils. She groaned with embarrassment. Flopping back on the floor, she hoped Quinn had slept through her drama queen moment. When a chuckle came from above she knew she was out of luck.

Quinn's head popped over the side of the mattress. "Morning, Rowan. You're one of those leap-out-of-bed types I see." His smothered laughter made her want to strangle him. He knew full well she hated mornings.

"You've just scared ten years off my life and you think it's funny?" Rowan tugged the sheet away from her legs and with as much dignity as she could manage, got to her feet and straightened her clothes. She wished she'd stayed on the floor when she looked at Quinn. Lying across the bed on his stomach with nothing but a strip of cloth covering his ass, he was every woman's wet dream come to life. Her slumbering coyote sat up, and Rowan breathed deep, only to suck in another lungful of Quinn's scent.

She fought to hold her beast back and remembered how hard it was when she'd learned to shift as a teenager. Using every trick she'd ever been taught, Rowan soothed the animal and held tight. Quinn needed to get dressed. In reality, it probably wouldn't make that much difference but every little bit helped.

"Get dressed," she growled between clenched teeth.

He scrambled out of bed, snatched his clothes from the floor and pulled them on without a protest. With all those muscles covered she would at least be able to look at him and pretend she was in control. Rowan eased back, unclenched her jaw and relaxed her arms and legs. Each small win over her coyote built her confidence, gained trust between her human and animal sides. But she needed to reward her coyote for behaving.

"I need to shift now. I'm in control, well as much as I can be at the moment, but I need to let her go."

"Okay, change. I'll be right here."

His unconditional support went a long way to soothing both her and her beast. Taking a deep breath, Rowan made her first intentional shift in six years.

The snap and pop of bones moving filled the room, the last of the changes not as loud or as painful as the first ones. It still took her longer than it should for a coyote her age but the time had shortened since yesterday. Then again, they'd changed together. The first three times had been the beast inside breaking free. Rowan felt more comfortable, more connected to her wild side than she had before and with one leap, her coyote bounded onto the bed.

Standing on four legs, she surveyed the room around her, absorbed the differences between now and when she was last here. Other than the bigger bed, the furniture was the same, even the quilt was the one handmade by her grandmother. Her gaze landed on Quinn. He'd changed, broadened across the chest a little. The lines beside his mouth and eyes could be from stress or laughter but they didn't detract from his appeal. They showed character and life. A life she hadn't been there to share.

The need for him to hold her surged through her, to feel the heart beating beneath his chest and his strong arms wrapped tightly around her. Shifting back came easier, the speed with which she took human form sucked the breath from her lungs and she fell forward only to be caught before she toppled off the bed. A wall of muscle lay against her cheek, the drumbeat on the other side soothed Rowan's need for closeness. The warm bands of muscle circling her back were like steel but she didn't feel restrained. Quinn's embrace was exactly what she needed.

They went from holding each other to devouring in seconds. Rowan had no idea who made the first move but when their lips connected it was like being struck by lightning. Every nerve sprang to attention and her blood rushed through her body, filling sensitive tissue to the point of bursting. Quinn's tongue lashed out, darted into her mouth to collide with hers. Rowan took all he offered and asked for more.

Teeth bumped and scraped along lips and tongues, and breath became secondary to taking in the man holding her. Lack of oxygen forced them apart but didn't stop the urge to take or the consuming need roaring to life inside her. They tumbled to the bed, legs entwined as hands pushed and pulled at clothing. From one breath to the next, Rowan's only goal was to get Quinn naked. To feel his skin against hers—to taste every inch of him.

Bare flesh met fingertips and she sighed with relief but craved more. Her hands molded every slope, every muscle, as they explored the changes in Quinn's body. So much was the same yet different. Hungry for more, Rowan followed her hands with her mouth. She skimmed his chest, stopped at one pebbled nipple to draw it in between her lips. She sucked hard and Quinn's hips thrust against her, his erection cradled by the softness of her stomach. Her hand traveled down his hard abs to delve inside his pants.

She wrapped her fingers around Quinn's cock, the hard length hot within her grasp. She stroked down to the root and cupped his balls before squeezing lightly. Mutual groans broke free as his sac pulled tight. Regaining her grip, she pulled her hand up to the tip, sweeping her thumb over the bead of moisture leaking from the slit. He pumped his hips and Rowan worked her hand up and down his rigid flesh, squeezing tighter with every thrust.

Desperation clawed at her. The passion neither of them had ever been able to deny exploded. She needed to taste him. To feel him inside her. Tugging at his remaining clothes, Rowan freed his cock and fought to move down his body. Quinn's hands circled her arms stopping her descent.

"No. Christ. You do that and I'm a goner," he panted.

"I don't care." She twisted to get free but his grip was strong and he flipped her beneath him to stop her struggles.

"Not this time."

He shoved her top under her arms with one hand and

lunged for her breasts. All protests died in her throat as he sucked a nipple into his mouth, swirled his tongue around the tip and scraped lightly with his teeth. Her back arched, more of her sensitive mound filling his mouth. He let her go, sat back and reached for the hem of her top. In a quick tug he had it up and off and flung across the room. Her pants followed.

Quinn proceeded to drive her wild. Touching and tasting her everywhere. No part of her was left out of his assault. Her nipples grew impossibly tight and her clit throbbed with arousal long ignored. The ecstasy bombarding her electrified her senses and aroused her coyote. Her beast stretched Rowan's control and forced her to clamp down on the delicious sensations Quinn's hands and mouth stirred. He pushed his leg between hers and spread her wide, exposing her for his wandering hand.

Fingers probed her slick folds. Sliding deeper, they teased her. Two fingers circled her opening before plunging deep. Her hips left the bed, propelled up with the decadent pleasure his invasion brought. His tongue continued to lavish attention on her breasts, swapping between them to give equal care. Quinn pressed down on her clit at the same time he stroked inside her core and Rowan's world shattered. With a scream she came. Her body thrashed as wave after wave of bliss rolled through her.

And her coyote broke free.

QUINN FELT Rowan's climax a second before she shifted. He threw himself to the side but wasn't quick enough to stop her claws from slicing into his scalp. The lacerations weren't deep and would heal without much bother but it would be one more reason for her to push him away. He knew her. She'd be devastated that she'd hurt him. Neither of them would come out of this unscathed and a few little scratches weren't anything he hadn't suffered before. Besides, he'd be damned if he'd let her do this alone.

Quinn's breath stalled in his throat as Rowan's coyote pounced on his chest. She licked his face and neck, nipped at his shoulder with her teeth. Her canines would leave welts but didn't break the skin. Frozen in place, he waited for the right moment to push her away. He didn't have a problem with getting it on in coyote form but they both had to be that way. Gently he placed a hand on her head, entwined his fingers in her fur and gave a small tug. When she turned to look at him Quinn took the opportunity to move out from under her and shift.

In his coyote form he nudged her with his snout and she quickly yielded to him. She rolled to her back, baring her stomach and throat, submitting to his alpha position. He was hard as granite and wanted desperately to claim his mate, but he fought his animal needs as he nuzzled her, using his tongue and teeth to soothe instead of arouse. If he gave in and took her now it would be a step backward in the path to control for Rowan. She needed his support and if that meant going without for now he'd do it.

It took some time and he had a few bite marks to show for it but she did settle, allowing him to take the time to look at her. Six years had changed her. The color of her coat was different —darker. Her physique was more muscular than it had been. Instead of a girl's body blossoming into womanhood, Rowan now had the curves of a mature woman and that change was evident in coyote form. Quinn longed to be able to explore every inch of her. He hadn't been able to do it before when they'd mated, but he'd do it now she was home. He'd learn all the parts of his mate.

Curled up together, they lay quietly, the occasional nip or

lick their only movements. Minutes passed and finally Rowan dozed. He waited a few more minutes before carefully removing himself from their tangle of limbs. Jumping from the bed he shifted back to his human body and scrambled back into his clothes, the more barriers between him and Rowan the better. Any extra time his common sense had to kick his brain into gear was a bonus.

He thought about waking her and then decided to leave her while he grabbed a shower. He could also take care of the not-so-little problem that was tenting his sweats. Quinn shook his head. Who was he kidding? Jerking off would only add to his troubles. Nothing would ease his condition but Rowan and there was no chance of that anytime soon. Sliding a drawer out slowly to minimize the noise, he searched out another pair of sweats and T-shirt. The jeans he'd had on yesterday could stay where they were in the bathroom until they went home.

Home.

Quinn didn't attempt to hold back the smile spreading across his face. To finally take Rowan home, as his mate, had been a dream he'd held close to his heart for over six long years. And now it was so close he could taste it. Stepping back over to the bed, he checked on the sleeping beauty who had held his heart for over a decade. A decade of pain and absence. What would the next ten years give them?

With Brogan as sovereign and Quinn by his side as regal, they stood to have it all. Once Rowan gained control of her animal side and they went home to Whispering Creek, there would be nothing standing in the way. They could live as mates the way they should have been from the start. He felt sure the pack would embrace her with open arms when she made her arrival home known. Until then he'd be the one with open arms.

· · ·

LIKE LAST NIGHT, the cold water did nothing to cool his arousal. He stepped from the shower the same way he'd entered it—his cock pointing the way. Dried and dressed, he checked on Rowan again before heading to the kitchen and food. They kept the cabin stocked with staples but he couldn't remember the last time they topped those supplies up. He found a packet of bacon in the freezer but no eggs in the fridge. The pantry did have a pancake mix though. He could whip those up while the bacon fried.

Quinn busied himself with breakfast preparations and a glance at the clock told him it was more like brunch but he wasn't getting into technicalities. The scent of bacon frying and coffee brewing filled the room. He lifted the last of the cooked bacon from the pan onto the plate and stashed it in the oven to keep warm while he made the pancakes. With fresh coffee now filling his cup, there wasn't much more he could ask for.

"Morning."

Ah...maybe one thing. He turned to find Rowan standing just inside the kitchen, barefoot and wearing another outfit similar to yesterday's. Her apprehension brought a flash of anger and he tamped it down quickly so he didn't worry her anymore. Why she'd be afraid of him now Quinn didn't have a clue. For the moment he'd ignore it and act as though this was any other normal day.

"Morning, Rowan. Breakfast is almost ready. Do you want a cup of coffee before we eat?" He moved to the pot, ready to pour her a cup when she stepped next to him.

"I can finish breakfast." She lifted the bowl of pancake batter from the counter.

"Oh no you don't." He snatched the bowl out of her hands and put it back down. "I'm cooking breakfast. You get to sit on that cute butt and watch." He steered her toward the table in the corner. Before she could protest, he had her in a chair.

Surprised by her easy acceptance, Quinn used it to his advantage and went back to fixing their meal. He poured Rowan a coffee, and remembering her comment about not taking sugar anymore, he left the brew black. Placing the mug on the table in front of her, he bent to brush his lips over hers. Ignoring the small jerk away his actions caused, he slid his tongue out and traced her lips from corner to corner. With a small amount of pressure she opened for him and he dipped inside to taste. A few quick licks and he pulled back, ending the kiss.

"Mmm...now that's a good morning."

"I'm sorry."

"For what?" He looked down at her, puzzled by her apology.

"For this morning when we were...well you know. I could have hurt you badly. I had no control over—."

He placed a finger on her lips, stopping any further words from spilling out. "Rowan, you did nothing wrong. Your coyote wanted her mate and I understand that. I'm fighting the same conflict inside, only I have more control at the moment. You have nothing to apologize for." He had no intention of telling her about the claw marks on his scalp but now he understood her timid behavior when she first came in. He didn't wait for her to comment. Turning back to the counter, he set about getting the pancakes cooked.

ROWAN SAT SIPPING HER COFFEE. Watching Quinn move around the kitchen with such ease was one more reminder of what she'd missed. When she'd left he couldn't tell the difference between a fry pan and a spatula. Now he not only knew the difference but how to use them and if the aroma filling the room was an indication, he used them well. He dropped batter into the pan, testing if it was ready before he turned it over. It looked easy but she knew from experience one had to judge the timing just right or you wrecked the pancake.

His sure competent movements spoke of familiarity and she supposed he'd gotten a lot of practice over the last six years. The muscles in his arms rippled with motion and the shirt molded to his back revealed more movement across his shoulder blades as he flipped another pancake. Her body heated, each nerve tingling with awareness as she absorbed the sight of Quinn. After this morning Rowan couldn't believe just looking at him had her turned on again.

The orgasm that had exploded through her had destroyed every bit of her control and let loose the animal who wanted only one thing. Her mate. She was shocked at what she'd done after shifting. They were lucky she hadn't hurt him with the way she'd been nipping at him with her sharp coyote teeth. When he'd managed to move her away and shift, she'd wanted nothing more than to turn her back and let him mount her but he hadn't let her. He'd kept her on her back and after she'd calmed down, let her roll to her side—curled beneath him. If she'd ever been unsure of his love, she was in no doubt now.

Quinn's behavior from the minute he'd slammed through the door yesterday had been nothing but loving and supportive. He may have tried to throw his weight around but he hadn't forced her to do anything but accept his presence and that wasn't such a hardship. The man was definitely worth looking at. And being taken care of wasn't so hard to stomach either. To have that after being without for so long brought tears to her eyes and a lump to her throat. The only person to give her that kind of support since she'd left home was El.

The move to Australia six years ago had been the best thing

she'd done in her attempt to stay hidden. Not only had she remained safe but she'd met El. God, she'd only left her two days ago and she missed her friend so much it was a physical ache. Quinn and Brogan would go a long way to soothing that pain but Rowan knew she and El would be friends forever. They were sisters of the heart and if it hadn't been for their friendship she knew without a qualm she never would have lasted this long away from home.

Quinn's hand on her chin startled her out of her thoughts. He tipped her face up and used his thumbs to wipe the tears from her cheek. Tears she hadn't known were falling.

"What's wrong? Why the silent tears?" The concern in his voice matched the emotion swirling in his eyes.

She shrugged. "It's all too much. I was thinking about us and how I've missed so much of your life."

"I've missed yours too, Rowan. We both lost a lot over the time you've been away but I plan to make up for it every day for the rest of our lives." He leaned forward, brushed a kiss on her temple, her cheek, her lips. "If you'll let me."

"Oh, Quinn." She wrapped her arms around his neck and pulled him close. She wanted to hold and be held. No, she needed it. Required the reassurance this was real and that she was in his arms and finally home.

"Shh...it's okay. Everything will be fine now you're home."

Rowan wanted to believe him. With all her heart she hoped he was right but there were still hurdles to overcome. She had to face the pack and explain her absence. Would they believe her when she told them of the threat to her safety? And what of the man hell-bent on having her to use her in his quest to become sovereign? Had he given up on his thirst to possess her now that Brogan had taken his rightful place in the pack or would she have another battle to fight after she'd gained control of her coyote?

If Marcus still wanted her as his mate, regardless of the fact they weren't destined to be together or that she and Quinn had mated, the battle wouldn't just be over her possession.

It would be for her life and Quinn's.

59

7

QUINN ADMIRED the way Rowan continued to face the challenges before her. He knew once she made herself known to the pack there would be more trouble. The council would want to know where she'd been and why she now wanted to return but they were the least of his concerns. She could handle the council and the rest of the pack for that matter, but he didn't know how she'd deal with facing Marcus after all these years.

Just thinking of him and what he'd done to Rowan had Quinn ready to kill. To rip the bastard to pieces.

He wished he and Brogan had been able to convince the council the man shouldn't be allowed to stay in the pack after they'd removed the senior Connelly, but until he did something worthy of exile they were stuck with him and all the problems he caused. If only Brogan had been sovereign at the time of Rowan's attack, it would have been easy to persuade the council then. They'd just have to be careful because if Quinn knew one thing it was that Marcus would do his best to stir up more trouble.

For now he'd concentrate on helping Rowan gain enough control to be comfortable with returning home. She might be on the mountain but this wasn't home. It was a safe harbor that could only last for so long. Anyone could discover she was back if they were in the forest for long. They needed to finish this so she could finally return to where she belonged. Judging by the speed with which she just shifted, it wouldn't be long before she'd be ready.

The late afternoon sun filtered through the trees surrounding the cabin, the dappled rays bouncing off the snow and sparkling in the puddles the warmth of the day had made. They'd been out here practicing for over two hours, Rowan shifting between coyote and human with ease now. As far as Quinn was concerned there was just one test left. They had to know if she could control the shift with him in close proximity because he had every intention of being by her side every minute of every day.

No time like the present to test her but they needed to be inside before he pushed. As much as he didn't think they were in any danger, he wanted them both safely locked indoors in case Rowan couldn't control the shift. He wouldn't think about his own control. The hard-on in his pants was a constant, one he'd managed to ignore for the most part. Tonight things would change. Once the sun went down he'd have her where he wanted her, under him.

He'd let her lead today, followed and allowed her to do things her way but now it was his turn. They both needed to know that she could control her coyote in any situation and seeing how he was responsible for three uncontrolled changes it would be a good test of her strength. The only problem was he was tested just as much with each minute he spent near her. Every second he didn't claim her, his body strained against his will to give her what she wanted and not take what he craved.

Rowan moved with a sensuality that had Quinn's insides humming. Each stretch of muscle, shift of skin to fur and back again, every smile she offered when she changed form with ease, had his coyote pulling to be let free. His nerves, as well as his control, were stretched tight. He wouldn't last much longer without having her. It was a good thing he wouldn't have to. If she shifted when she came tonight he'd change and claim her coyote.

Tonight would be the end of this torture he was enduring. Rowan wasn't fairing much better. He knew by the way she looked at him her arousal was high. He didn't need the taut nipples showing through her tank top or the way her breath hitched and she licked her lips when he caught her looking at him as confirmation. The flush on her cheeks wasn't just from exertion either. He might not be able to see because of the shirt she wore but he'd bet anything her breasts glowed with the same rosy hue as her cheeks.

Aching with need, his cock throbbed in his pants. Eager to see Rowan's flushed skin beneath him, Quinn jumped to his feet and stalked toward her. She froze in place, wide eyed as she watched him approach. Her sharp intake of air and labored breathing told him she knew his intentions. He stopped two feet away, afraid to get any closer for fear he'd take her here and now.

"Enough for today," he growled, his voice gravelly with the lust riding his back. "We're moving inside. It's time to take this one step further."

Rowan's eyes widened farther and her nostrils flared as she sucked in a breath. With only a nod, she stepped around him and raced toward the house. Quinn closed his eyes and took a deep breath, giving her time to lock him out if she wanted. He knew she wouldn't but he'd give her that option anyway. It also gave him a moment to regain control of the beast currently howling to take what was his. If they came together right now he wouldn't be gentle and he wanted their first time after so long to be about their love, not their animal need to mate.

He sighed. Was there even a difference? He didn't know if he could separate the two but he'd be damned if he'd take her like an animal this first time.

ROWAN CLOSED the bathroom door but didn't turn the lock. Shutting it would keep Quinn out. She trusted him to respect her need for privacy. Not that she wanted to stay away from him. A few minutes to freshen up and calm down were all she sought. Her nerves tingled with expectation and her coyote howled with excitement. To finally be in Quinn's arms after all this time seemed surreal. On the one hand, it was as natural as breathing, but on the other, she was terrified.

Terrified of all he made her feel, all they were to each other. Time and distance hadn't dulled what was between them and she hoped she'd managed to master her coyote and merged her two sides completely. Relief at reaching this point flowed through her. Tense shoulders relaxed and the ache in her heart eased. That told her how much being with him but not *being* with him affected her. The strain of holding back, of not touching even when all she wanted was to brush her fingers along his arm in passing. The fear of hurting him if her coyote broke free was enough to have her taking a wide berth around him at all times. After tonight there would be no need for such care.

Today had proven she had the ability to control her coyote with ease now they'd gotten reacquainted. While she'd concentrated on perfecting her shift, Quinn had sat and watched.

Never once did he interfere or approach her. She knew what he planned now that she'd gained confidence and she anticipated it with an eagerness that thrummed through her. The sooner they got started the better. But first she wanted a shower. Shifting back and forth had worked up a sweat that clung to her skin.

She stripped off her clothes and stepped into the shower cubicle. The large space allowed her room to stand back out of the water as she waited for the hot to come through. Goose bumps covered her flesh but quickly vanished as the steam rose and she slipped beneath the showerhead. Her shoulder-length hair stuck to her neck in strands, rivulets of water trailing from each end. Eyes closed tight, she turned her face under the spray and allowed the warmth to cascade over her.

Not wanting to take too long, she shampooed her hair and washed her body in record time. Showering had always been an indulgence but now she had other decadent treats to pursue. Or treat. The giggle that bubbled up her throat both surprised and thrilled her. Pleasure had been a rare event in the past few years. Always the nagging fact that she couldn't return home weighed on her mind and stopped her from enjoying the simplest of things.

She had stayed away not only to protect herself but Quinn. Rowan worried not enough time had passed for Marcus to have moved on. Still, she refused to remain apart from Quinn any longer. Doing so had worn her down, torn her apart. Marcus had stolen so much from them. No more would she allow her sorrow to cloud her days—or nights. Now she would embrace all that life had to offer with an open heart and mind.

Starting with Quinn.

Rowan shut off the water and reached for a towel. Brisk movements had her body dry so she wouldn't drip all over the floor. She used a second towel to wrap around her head, squeezing hard to soak up the excess water from her hair. Satisfied, she removed the towel and slid it over the hanging rail. It was then Rowan realized she hadn't brought clean clothes in with her. There were two options. Use a towel to cover herself or walk out naked and hope Quinn wasn't waiting on the other side of the bathroom door. It wasn't like he hadn't seen her naked before anyway.

She took a deep breath and cracked open the door to peer through the gap. There was no sign of Quinn but she could hear him in the kitchen. Flinging the door wide, she raced across the small hall to the bedroom. About four feet by four feet square, the hall basically comprised of three doors and an opening that led to the living area. The bathroom door stood between the two bedrooms so she only had to dash half the distance before making it to the relative safety of the bedroom.

The curse that met her ears as she crossed the threshold told her she hadn't been quick enough. Heavy footsteps and a growl followed her into the room. With a lightness she hadn't felt in far too long, she darted to the far side of the bed and turned to face her mate. Quinn's chest rose and fell in sharp, ragged breaths, his nostrils flared and his eyes blazed with desire. A shiver traveled the length of her spine and ripples of pleasure skittered over her skin.

He looked at her with such need it took her breath and tightened her insides. Her instincts made her yearn to lie on the bed and give him whatever he wanted, but it warred with her own needs and wants. Nerve endings pulsed, sending sensation throughout her body, no part of her left unaffected. Her breasts grew heavy and the nipples puckered into hard nubs. The heat building between her legs beat with the rhythm pounding in her ears. Liquid arousal pooled in her pussy, coating her slit and inner thighs.

Quinn moved and her heart jumped. Like earlier in the

yard, he stalked her, hunted her down like prey. Far from being scared, Rowan reveled in the excitement his actions brought. Held in place by his hypnotizing stare, she waited. He reached her before her next breath and the thrill of standing before him naked while he remained fully clothed shot aching need into her core. A stuttered breath caught in her chest and left her breathless.

Caught between the urge to act and the wish to submit to his every whim, Rowan stood transfixed, mesmerized. Her body trembled with longing when Quinn raised one hand to trail his fingertips lightly over her stomach, up between her breasts and under her chin. Tilting her face until their gazes met, he studied her with such intent that her insides quaked. His head lowered, bringing his mouth to hers. Lips brushed, pulled back, moved forward. Her eyes fluttered closed.

"Are you ready for me, Rowan?" Quinn spoke against her mouth.

Her eyes popped open and staring into his, she gave the slightest of nods.

Her world spun as Quinn lifted her from the floor and turned. Her stomach dropped as he threw them both on the bed. His weight pressed into her, trapping her between his hard body and the soft bedding. Rowan didn't get a chance to catch the breath that flew from her lungs. Quinn's mouth took hers in a savage kiss that burned all thought of breathing away.

Their tongues dueled, each forcing their way inside the other to taste and take. Yielding, she allowed him to control the kiss. Aching with want, her hands began to roam his body. Frustration at finding the barrier between his skin and her fingers brought a growl to her throat. She tugged at his clothes, bit his lip to get his attention. Quinn surged back, separating their mouths, each of them left gasping for breath.

"Clothes. Off. Now." Each word was spoken on a ragged puff of air.

He pushed to his knees, straddling her hips. As she shoved his shirt up, he gripped the hem and yanked it over his head, tossing it aside. Her hands were already working on removing his pants without much luck. Another frustrated growl rent the air but this time it was Quinn's. A quick roll to the side and he had his pants past his hips and off. Before she could take advantage of his exposed position, he flipped back over on top of her.

Hot skin met hot skin. Rowan moaned in delight. Quinn's answering groan filled her mouth as he thrust his tongue between her lips. Taking the kiss deep, he took her on a carnal ride that ignited fire in her veins. Lust exploded between them. Hands searched and found sensitive flesh, delivering spikes of pleasure throughout her body. Mouths meshed, tongues stroked and teeth nipped. Cream flowed from her core, spreading slick heat between her legs.

She parted her thighs allowing Quinn's hips to slip between them. His erection nestled along her sex and ground against her clit. Her pussy clenched. Rowan bent her knees and wrapped her legs around his waist. Heals digging into his ass, she pulled him down as she surged up, their pelvises locked together. Ecstasy burst through her and she began to rock against him. Coated in her juices, his cock slid across her swollen folds and pushed her closer to the orgasm just out of reach.

Quinn's lips left hers to trace a line of kisses over her jaw and down her neck. He licked and nibbled his way toward her breasts. His tongue swirled around one sensitive nub before sucking it between his lips. Drawing hard, he pressed the taut peak to the roof of his mouth. Her hips rocked faster and more fluid seeped from her convulsing channel. It wasn't enough.

The climax she needed taunted her with its closeness. Her head thrashed on the bed and her body undulated beneath his, trying to grab hold of what she craved.

Raw desire flooded her body, made her frantic to get what she wanted. Quinn continued to work her breasts, feasting on each nipple in turn. His teeth scraped the inflamed points. Electric darts exploded from the slight pain, delivering yet more fragmented need to the tender tissues lining her pussy. Rowan grabbed Quinn's hips, tilted her own until the head of his cock was lined up with her opening, arching up she forced his flesh into hers. His mouth left her breast and she cried out at the loss.

"God, Rowan, stop," he panted.

Her answer was to push higher, take a little more of him inside.

"Slow down." His words were harsh on each jagged breath. "Want it to last."

Slow down? Was he insane? She'd die if she didn't feel him embedded in her fully. Rowan rolled her hips, slid her slick heat farther onto his shaft. His cock jerked against her as the tight fit gave them both immense pleasure. Quinn growled.

"Damn it, Rowan."

He tried to withdraw but with her hands on his hips and her legs hugging his waist she followed.

"I wanted slow and easy this first time."

"No," she gasped. "Hard and fast. Now."

Using her arms and legs she thrust up, lifted off the bed and impaled herself on his cock.

QUINN'S CONTROL SNAPPED.

Like the crack of a whip, it echoed in his mind and his body moved. Thought fled and instinct took over. Arms curled under her back, he wrapped his hands around her shoulders. His fingers dug into her soft skin in a death grip that left his knuckles white. Flexing his hips he withdrew from her clasping sheath and slammed back in. Withdraw. Advance. Withdraw. Advance. The rhythm hard and fast, exactly what she'd asked for. What his body craved.

Wet slapping noises filled the air, mingled with the scent of arousal to make a potent aphrodisiac to their already over-stimulated senses. She met him thrust for thrust. Pounding in and out of the tight vise of her body, Quinn knew only one thing. Rowan. His coyote howled as he claimed his mate and Quinn grunted with every lunge forward. With each pass along her rippling channel her body jerked beneath his, restricted by his weight, her movements minimal. The hot slide of his cock on her moist flesh sent fire shooting into his balls and up his spine.

Quickening his pace, Quinn powered his hips, the soft curves of her ass cushioning each blow his thighs made when they connected. He tucked his head to latch his mouth around a nipple. Suckling the hard tip, he used his teeth to scrape the tender bud. Rowan bucked and thrashed, her pussy contracting around his cock. Her quivering walls milked him, made his balls squeeze tight. He drove into her, ground his pubic bone against her clit and set off an explosion.

She erupted under him. Her pussy clamped hard, held tight to his shaft. He dragged his length out and surged back in. He rode her, pistoned in and out of her pulsing flesh until the fireball in his groin took him. Molten lava roared through him and burst free to spill in Rowan's core. No part of him went unscorched. Every muscle rigid as he strained against her, buried to the hilt in her writhing body. Exhausted, Quinn collapsed on top of her.

Sweat dripped down his forehead, coated his skin and pooled between them. Their chests slid as they pulled in great gulps of air in an attempt to satisfy oxygen-starved lungs. He tingled from head to toe and was sure he'd see stars if he opened his eyes. Rowan squirmed beneath him and his cock twitched with renewed life. Still locked inside her depths, Quinn felt the last of her orgasm subside. Each squeeze of muscle a tantalizing reminder of the peak they'd just ascended.

With the little energy he had left, Quinn rolled to the side. He took Rowan with him until they lay in reverse. Her splayed on top of him. His erection, still semi-hard in spite of the climax he'd just had, slid to leave only the head breaching her opening. Rowan moaned and her pussy fluttered, the grip on the sensitive gland at the crown hardened his shaft further. Her nipples prodded his ribs as she rocked her hips, the roll allowing his cock to slide in then out of her. He groaned. She moved again.

Hands on her hips, Quinn turned her rock into a thrust. Stroke after stroke, he bucked up into her willing body. Slow and steady, he moved within her, drawing it out, taking his time to love her. Her walls held him like a glove. Warm and wet, he slid along rippling muscles, their combined cum lubricating the way. His fingers pressed into the flesh of her ass, kneading the cheeks, he pulled her up and down his erection faster. She spread her palms on his chest and bracing her arms, sat astride him.

The angle of penetration changed, rubbing sensitive spots, eliciting moans from both of them. Rising to her knees, Rowan began to ride him. Slow slide up, fast drop down. She set a rhythm that teased. The pace remained unhurried, and Quinn enjoyed the vision before him. Back arched, head thrown back, she rode him. She took them both on a leisurely journey to paradise. Unlike the frenzied, breathless rush of their first coupling, this unhurried pace satisfied his initial intention of a slow, thorough loving.

Rowan's breasts bounced with her movements and he

couldn't resist cupping them in his palms. He curled his fingers and molded her supple flesh, testing the weight and brushing her nipples with a sweep of his thumbs. The little cries of delight slipping from her throat spurred him on and he pinched the buds until they puckered tight. Their dark brown color looked like drops of chocolate on her creamy skin. Surging up, he sucked first one and then the other between his lips.

Coated in his saliva, they sparkled. With finger and thumb he pulled and pinched one while his mouth went to work on its twin. He opened his jaw wide, sucked in as much as he could and flicked his tongue across the peak. She thrust her chest into his face, forced more of her mound past his lips. Greedy, he took what she offered. Pulling back, he scraped his teeth gently along her skin. When he got to her nipple he bit harder and tugged. Her pussy tightened around his cock and she rode him faster.

He reached between them, used his fingers to locate the bundle of nerves at the top of her slit. The bud, already popped from its protective hood, was covered in slick cream. Circling the nub, he kept his tempo in time with hers. If she sped up so did he. When she slowed down, he did too. Rowan soon worked out his actions and took advantage. With a skill that came from her sensual nature, she used him to take her over the edge. She bucked and rolled her pelvis, drawing him with her on her way to the top.

It started with tiny quivers and turned into clasping spasms. Her climax rushed through her. Her muscles convulsed in a rolling motion, from the base of his cock to the tip, they surrounded him. He felt the burn in his balls as he hit the peak and went over. His sac pulled up tight and shot cum through his shaft like a bullet from a gun, the recoil jolting his hips. A grunt escaped around the breast in his mouth and he let it go to pull Rowan's face to his, claiming her lips in a breath stealing kiss as the last of his seed spilled deep inside her.

Quinn cupped her head in his hands and staring into her eyes, he said the words he'd waited what seemed like a lifetime to say.

"Welcome home, Rowan."

8

HOME.

Rowan's exhausted body sprang to life. She could go home to Whispering Creek.

Now.

A smile stretched her lips and laughter bubbled in her chest. Excitement fizzed in her veins and her head spun with the thrill of finally getting her most precious wish. Home. She was going home.

She smacked her lips to Quinn's, kissed him hard before raising her hips and letting his spent cock slip from her body. The friction sent a delicious shiver along her pussy walls, adding to the happiness bombarding her. Bounding off the bed, she danced around the room, laughing and cheering. And crying. Tears streamed down her face and dripped from her chin but she didn't care. Nothing mattered right now. She could leave the cabin. *They* could leave.

Rowan spun around and rummaged in a drawer for something to wear. She threw on the first sweatshirt she found. Quinn's scent surrounded her and her libido jumped. Damn it was good to be with him. Smiling, she dragged on a pair of shorts. Pulling another set of pants and shirt from the drawer she tossed them over her shoulder and toward the bed. A muffled curse met her ears. Twirling in circles, she continued to laugh and cry, only stopping when she got too dizzy to spin anymore.

"What are you doing?"

"I can go home!" Her words came out as a high-pitched squeal.

"What, now?" He arched an eyebrow.

"Yes, now!" Arms out wide, she whirled around once more.

"God, Rowan, can't we wait until morning?"

"No. I've waited six years, Quinn. With every breath, every thought, I've wished for this moment and now it's here." Breathless with excitement, she jumped on the bed beside him. Grabbing his hand, she wove her fingers with his. "Don't you see? We can go home. Together."

Quinn brought their joined hands to his lips. He feathered light kisses on each knuckle before turning her hand over and kissing her palm. Tiny shockwaves of electricity fired up her wrist and into her arm. The tingle of arousal darted off in all directions when the sensation met her shoulder. She trembled.

"If that's what you want, we'll go." He squeezed her hand and let it go. "But we better hurry up. If we're going I don't want to leave too late. We're supposed to get a snowstorm overnight."

"Really? I love snowstorms. I can't remember the last one I saw." Rowan's mind ticked back through the years, all the way back to her last winter in the mountains. For a moment, sadness descended but she soon snapped out of it when Quinn rolled off the bed. She'd vowed not to let the past cloud her future and she was damn well going to be sure she didn't.

"I'll grab our dirty laundry while you dress, it won't take a second and we'll be ready to leave."

Rowan left the bedroom and picked up the clothes hamper in the bathroom before making her way to the living area. Quinn was already pulling on his boots. A shiver traveled up her spine at the sight of muscle flexing in his arms as he tugged the work boots over bare feet. Her skin prickled with awareness and her heart rate increased. You'd think they hadn't gone at it like animals ten minutes ago. The man turned her on just being in the room. She tried to swallow, her mouth and throat suddenly dry as dirt making it difficult.

"Ready?" she croaked.

He reached for the laundry as he stood. "Yep, let's get going."

They made their way out to Rowan's rental car. It was a good thing they were leaving now. There was no way the little hatchback would make it down the mountain if the predicted snowfall was a heavy one. Quinn pulled the keys from his pocket and she wondered when he collected them. For that matter she couldn't remember when she'd last had them, lucky he was on the ball. Early evening chill surrounded them and they quickly got in the car, Quinn starting it and cranking the heater up. Rowan shuddered as the first blast of air came out cold.

"Give it a second and it'll warm up. It won't take long to get to the house and Brogan will have the furnace going."

The ride along the mountain road took about fifteen minutes. With each passing second Rowan became more and more excited and by the time they turned up the drive to the house she was bouncing on her seat. She soon stopped when the log structure came into view. The long sweeping front porch, the wide double-entry doors, the second-floor windows and the shingled roof looked exactly how she remembered them. She held her breath, afraid it was all a dream and she'd wake up to find it all a lie.

"Fuck."

Quinn's curse jarred her out of her thoughts. Turning to look at him, she found his fingers gripped the wheel so tight his knuckles had turned white. A muscle ticked in his jaw and he stared at the house with anger. Rowan looked back at the house but couldn't work out what was wrong other than the big four-wheel drive parked right in the middle of the driveway.

"Does Brogan have visitors?"

"An unwelcome one, yes," Quinn forced out between clenched teeth.

"Well that's okay, we can just leave him—"

"No. It's not okay." He turned to face her and Rowan's heart pounded. "The owner of that truck is someone I don't want you near. Ever. We'll drive around for a while and come back."

"Don't be silly, Quinn. Why can't we go inside and what do you mean by you don't want me near them?" Sweat broke out on her skin and she wished with all she was he didn't say the one name she knew would come out of his mouth.

"Marcus."

She sucked in a breath, held it tight and tried to calm her galloping heart. Marcus couldn't hurt her. Not like last time. She wouldn't let him get close enough ever again. With effort, she willed her muscles to relax, her pulse to slow. Each labored draw of air into her lungs eased as she looked at Quinn.

"I won't let him touch you. I'll kill him if he does."

His vow was one she could see in his eyes. Without doubt she knew he'd back up his words with actions. As they sat in the dark of the car, the motor vibrating under the hood and the heater blasting warm air onto their faces, Rowan made a personal vow. She would not allow Marcus to take any more from her. Wouldn't let him destroy what had taken years to rebuild. She was stronger now, no longer a scared teenager but a grown woman prepared to fight for what was hers. Quinn. Her home. Her destiny.

Rowan reached over and cupped his cheek. "You won't need to kill anyone, Quinn. He wouldn't hurt me again. I wouldn't let him." She stroked her fingers along his stubble-covered jaw. "As much as I don't want to see him, I'm going in. That's my home and I have a right to be there. He won't keep me from it, or you, ever again."

Taking a deep breath, she wrapped her fingers around the door handle and waited for Quinn to turn off the engine. This was where it really began. Coming home and gaining control of her coyote had been the easy part. Facing her demons would take everything she'd learned over the past six years. It would also take courage and strength. She'd had neither as a teenager, both attributes had developed over time and she was more than ready to use them to claim what was hers.

QUINN COULDN'T BELIEVE their luck. Of all the bad timing, he had to go and pick this one to drive into. Rowan had to face Marcus at some point but he'd hoped to put it off as long as possible. The reality was they were getting the first meeting over with now. He hated to see the happiness fade from her eyes and be replaced by fear. She'd been so excited before they pulled into the driveway. With spine straight, shoulders back and chin thrust forward she sat waiting for him to turn the car off and get out.

The fear had been replaced by a stubborn, determined glint. He knew that look, it was the one she had when she was prepared to get what she wanted. And right now she wanted to go home and he would make sure she got her wish with the least amount of trouble. Even if it meant he had to toss Marcus out of the house on his ear.

A flick of his wrist and the engine died. Sudden silence filled the car. Quinn hopped out and jogged around to help Rowan get her footing. The sight of her bare feet had him laughing.

"Forget something?" he asked as he slid one arm behind her back and the other under her knees.

"Put me down, Quinn. I can walk."

"You'll freeze your toes off on the snow. I'll put you down on the porch."

Why hadn't he noticed she'd left the cabin without shoes? His long strides ate up the ground, he took the steps two at a time and had just put her on her feet when the front door flew open and Brogan charged out to pull her into a hug, her toes dangling off the ground. He was about to suggest going inside when a voice broke the quiet.

"Well, well, well, if it isn't the return of the prodigal bitch, alive and well."

The snarl Quinn issued through his teeth was matched by Brogan. Taking a step forward, he was stopped by a gentle touch on his arm.

"Hello, Marcus, I didn't see you there." Rowan's voice held no trace of animosity toward the man who'd destroyed so much of her life.

Marcus ignored her, turned his attention to Quinn. "Finally managed to leash the bitch I see."

Quinn saw red. He'd rip the man's throat out for referring to her in such a derogatory manner. The hand on his arm gripped harder, fingers and nails digging in to stop him. Rowan was right to stop him. He couldn't afford to do anything stupid, not before or after she made herself known to the council and the pack members. Reining in his anger, Quinn tried to remember who the better man was but with his coyote howling to take down the threat to his mate, it proved a difficult task. The sneer that curled Marcus's lips was almost his undoing.

"Or is it the big bad regal who's been leashed?"

Marcus didn't know when his life was in jeopardy but then Quinn had never believed the man had more than one active brain cell. And right now his mouth was using it.

"Weren't you leaving?" Brogan asked.

"Yes, I have better places to be than at a sickly sweet family reunion." Marcus pushed past, shouldering Quinn in the chest as he went.

Rowan's nails dug into his skin. "Don't," she whispered. "He's not worth it."

She was right of course but damn if he wouldn't enjoy taking the bastard out. No one said a word as they watched Marcus jump in his truck and rev the engine. He peeled out of there, sprayed the drive and the far end of the porch with snow and slush as he swung the back end around and headed down the drive. Quinn breathed easy when the truck was out of sight. He didn't for one minute think that would be the end of it but for now Rowan was safe.

He draped his arm over Rowan's shoulders and turned them back to the door. "Come on, let's get in out of the cold and welcome you home properly."

Brogan closed the door behind them, taking his time to lock all the deadbolts. Something they didn't do very often. That alone told Quinn how concerned for Rowan's safety her brother was. Catching Brogan's eye, they let Rowan go ahead of them. When Quinn felt she was out of earshot he asked the question he'd wanted to ask the second he'd seen Marcus's truck.

"What did Marcus want?"

"He came to inform me of an official complaint he filed with the council."

"What the hell has he cooked up against you this time?" Quinn kept an eye on the door Rowan had disappeared through.

"Actually this time he's gone for you."

His gaze jerked back to Brogan. "What?"

"He's claiming you killed Rowan in a lovers rage and buried her in the mountains somewhere."

Quinn's jaw dropped—his mind blank. This latest challenge to their positions as sovereign and regal left him speechless.

"You know I'm just going to make you two repeat whatever it is you're saying once you get in here so you may as well come in and start over now before you get too far into it," Rowan yelled from the living room.

Brogan rolled his eyes. "Damn, it's good to have her back." He slapped Quinn on the back. "Come on, let's go satisfy her curiosity."

ROWAN KNEW whatever Marcus was here for hadn't been good. Brogan had worry lines creasing his brow and Quinn looked like he'd been punched in the stomach. Apprehension skittered down her spine and she waited for one of them to start talking.

In the end, she had to ask. Neither of them was forthcoming with the information and the longer they delayed the less time they had to work out how to deal with the problem.

"Okay, enough with the silent treatment. One of you needs to start talking now." She gave them both her best intimidating stare.

"Marcus has gone to the council with the accusation that

Quinn killed you in a lover's argument and buried your remains in the mountains." Brogan looked from her to Quinn and back again. "He says he knows where you're buried too."

The quaking started low in her belly, vibrated up into her chest until it forced its way up her throat and burst from her mouth. Arms wrapped around her waist, Rowan doubled over and laughed herself stupid.

"Why the hell are you laughing? He's accused Quinn of murder." Brogan's voice rose above her hilarity.

When she couldn't catch her breath to form a word she gave up and flopped back on the couch to let the mirth die a natural death. Unlike her. She hadn't died at all. More giggles spilled out and Quinn sat next to her patting her on the back as if she was choking. By the time she'd calmed down, Brogan had sat in the seat opposite.

"Can't either of you see how funny this is?" Her head swiveled back and forth, taking in both their troubled expressions. "For a start he'd have to produce a body and he's gonna look pretty stupid when that body shows up breathing."

Her revelation didn't appease them. Sighing, she slumped back into the cushion. Rowan really couldn't see why they were so concerned. All she had to do was turn up in town tomorrow morning and prove Marcus wrong.

Quinn's quiet words broke the silence. "You showing up only proves I didn't kill you, it doesn't prove we didn't fight or that I didn't hurt you seriously enough to warrant your disappearance. The council will still want to investigate the allegations fully and while they're doing that and occupying my time and energy, Marcus will be trying something else."

"If we've learned one thing about Marcus in the last few years, it's that he's predictable. He always starts something and uses it as a smoke screen for what he's really after," Brogan said.

"But why would he accuse Quinn now, after all this time?"

"I don't know, but the more I think about it the more I realize Marcus wasn't at all surprised to see you. Which makes me think he knew you were here."

"He could have picked up her scent in the forest the same as I did," Quinn said.

"Hmm. You might be right. He was looking around like he expected someone else to come into the room the whole time he was here." Brogan rubbed his hand across the back of his neck, a sign Rowan remembered from her youth. He was frustrated at not knowing all the answers.

She stifled a yawn. The warmth of the room seeped into her bones and muscles and made her drowsy. Cuddling into Quinn's side, she relaxed and let her eyelids drift shut. Continuing their discussion on Marcus, Rowan listened with half an ear, only adding the odd word here or there. Her knowledge of Marcus was limited by the time she'd spent away from the pack and before that she'd had very little to do with him.

Quinn had pulled her in under his arm and gave her a squeeze when she yawned for about the tenth time.

"I think we should call it a night and start fresh in the morning. Rowan's tired and needs to rest," Quinn said.

"There isn't really that much we can do anyway. We've been talking in circles for a while and still haven't come up with a decent idea." Brogan pushed from his chair. "I'll check everything is locked up tight before going to bed."

Brogan leaned down and brushed a kiss across her forehead. "It's great to have you home, Sis. Sleep well and I'll see you both in the morning."

Rowan watched him leave the room. Another yawn split her mouth wide and cracked her jaw.

Quinn chuckled. "Come on sleepyhead, let's get you into bed." Like he had out at the car, he picked her up and carried her. He stopped near the door. "Flick the light off for me, my hands are full."

Doing his bidding, Rowan snuggled in to enjoy the ride up to her room. Only they didn't go to her old room, they went to the bigger one at the back of the house. Depositing her on the king-size bed, Quinn switched on a bedside lamp, illuminating the room. It was clearly stamped with his personality and hers. All the mementos she'd left behind had been moved in here.

The photo of her parents on their wedding day sat on the dresser. The gold frame that held her cherished picture of Quinn sat next to it. Her jewelry box, a gift from her mother, held prime position on the tallboy in the corner and when he opened a drawer of the dresser and removed one of her favorite sleeping shirts, Rowan couldn't hold back the tears.

9

NOW THAT HER crying jag had calmed to the odd hiccup, Rowan nestled into Quinn's side. He hadn't said a word when the dam burst. He'd wrapped her in his arms and let the storm blow over. Drained, both physically and mentally, she soaked up his warmth—basked in the glory of being loved by this man. If she put everything aside, her destiny to hold the position of royal, his role in pack leadership and them being mates, she would still love him. Before she ever knew what romantic love was she'd been in love with Quinn.

He'd been a part of her for so long—longer than she could remember. Leaving him behind had left a hole in her that gaped and oozed like an open wound. From the moment he'd crashed back into her life the gash began to heal. Each second that passed eased the pain a little more. Surrounded by all she'd known and loved in her youth, and with her future stretched out in front of her, Rowan felt at peace for the first time in her adult life.

She didn't think her worries were over but she wouldn't let them stand in her way again. Maturity and absence had made her heart and mind stronger and she planned to take charge of her world one step at a time. She'd made headway with her coyote, she'd faced her fear of Marcus with surprising ease and when it came time to front the council, Rowan would be more than ready.

Quinn's hand traveled in lazy circles on her lower back. The soothing motion sent conflicting sensations throughout her body. The light, comforting strokes lulled her into sleep but the tingle of skin on skin when his fingers grazed beneath her shirt sent darts of awareness to every nerve ending. A shiver skipped along her spine and trembled to the tips of her fingers and toes. Arousal swirled low in her belly, hardened her nipples and wet her core.

Rowan slung a leg over his and pushed her throbbing center against his hip in the hope of relief. A spark of electricity shot into her clit and her inner muscles clenched. Cream soaked her panties. Quinn's arm tightened and his hand stopped. For a moment not a breath was taken. Time froze and the world stilled as they lay there. One heartbeat. Two. Then Quinn moved and nothing else mattered.

His tongue invaded her mouth and conquered. He stole her breath and gave it back again. The hand on her back had moved to her ass, splayed fingers cupping one cheek. Other clever digits teased her breast, plying a nipple until it beaded tight. Rowan's hands weren't idle either. They pulled and tugged at clothing. Groped at muscles rippling under smooth skin and teased sensitive flesh. Moans, muffled by their joined mouths, filled the air.

The heady scent of desire cloaked them, pushed them higher. Quinn tore his mouth from hers, dragged his lips over her chin and down her throat. His teeth scraped across her skin, goose bumps trailing in their wake. He sucked at her neck, hard enough to leave a mark. The tinge of pain mixed with pleasure fizzed in her veins, pumped through her to pound in her core. Rowan's pussy convulsed, moisture seeping from within to heat folds slick with need. Surging up, she ground her sex against his side.

Quinn growled and yanked free of her hold. In one quick move, he ripped his shirt over his head and dropped it on the floor beside the bed. Rowan scrambled to do the same. When he reached for her pants, sliding his fingers in the waistband she didn't protest. Lifting her hips to help, she was soon stripped bare. With greedy hands, she helped him remove the rest of his clothes before reaching to envelop his cock in her fist.

Hard and hot, it jerked in her grasp. Long, firm strokes from root to tip and back again had him groaning. Pre-cum beaded at the slit and Rowan leaned forward to swipe it off with her tongue. His hand cupped the side of her head, fingers tangled in her hair and tugged her closer. She took the hint and opened her mouth to suck the mushroom tip inside. Swirling her tongue, she teased the sensitive gland. He growled in approval and his fingers curled—dug into her scalp.

Flavor exploded on her tongue. The scent of musky male arousal filled her nostrils, saturated her senses. Hungry for more of his taste, Rowan slid his shaft between her lips. She closed her mouth around him and sucked hard. Cheeks hollowing, she pulled him deeper, flicking her tongue along his length as she did. He thrust his hips, driving into her mouth. The plump head nudged the back of her throat and she swallowed around it, fought the urge to gag.

Quinn loosened his hold on her head and withdrew from her mouth. Rowan greedily slurped at his cock as it slipped free. He pushed her to her back, put his hands on her thighs and spread her legs wide. Dipping his head, he took a deep breath before blowing a stream of warm air over her clit. Her body jolted, electrified by the sudden stimulation. With a sweep of his tongue, he laved her from back to front.

He devoured her. With teeth, tongue and lips, he ate at her, sent her rocketing toward orgasm and over the edge in minutes. Spasms racked her from head to toe, her hips bucking beneath his ravishing mouth. There was no time to come down. Quinn took her back up to the peak before surging over her and penetrating her in one hard thrust. Her walls clamped, held tight to his cock. Buried to the hilt, he stilled, pelvis locked to pelvis.

Frustrated with need, Rowan contracted her muscles, squeezing along his length. He flexed his hips; the base of his shaft brushed her clit and sent a barrage of intense craving to her core. She wrapped her legs around his thighs, dug her hands into his ass and arched her back to urge him to move. When that didn't work she sank her teeth into his shoulder.

"Move, dammit!"

"Not yet. Don't want to come too soon," he panted.

Rowan growled and thrashed under him. His cock slid from her pussy, hitting her G-spot and sending sparks of delight into her belly. She drove her hips up off the bed and plunged onto his erection again, her muscles quaking with lust. Quinn's cock pulsed as he rammed into her, slamming home hard. Every inch of delicate tissue was stimulated beyond measure. He withdrew, plunged forward, withdrew. In and out, he took them both to new heights.

Back and forth, they rocked together, each movement harsher than the last. Frantic, savage actions brought them closer to release. Nails and teeth bit into flesh, dragged across sweat slick skin. Grunts and groans rebounded off walls, echoed in her ears and competed with the slap of wet bodies colliding. Quinn's hands curled over her hips, his fingers dug in and pinned her in place as he pumped into her. Clawing at his back, Rowan dug her heels into the bed and tried to meet him thrust for thrust.

Caught in his strong grip, she strained against him. Head thrown back, Rowan pushed her breasts into Quinn's chest. Taut nipples prodded hard muscle. Coarse hair abraded the tender buds, they puckered tighter and electric pulses of need beat through her to center in her core. She bent her knees, flung her legs around his waist to lock her ankles together and pull him closer. Her pelvis titled, her ass lifted off the bed and his cock stroked in deeper. Pounding in and out, the mushroom head brushed her G-spot with each slide.

Quinn's teeth clamped down on her nipple at the exact moment he drove balls deep and ground his pubic bone hard against her clit. Fire burst inside her and stars exploded in front of her eyes. Her body went rigid, every muscle frozen in that split second before she shattered into a million pieces. The world narrowed to nothing but the ecstasy flooding her senses. She called his name, a rasp of sound that was barely heard over Quinn's cry of release.

Clutched within her, his cock jerked and spilled a pool of warmth as he emptied his seed. Her walls continued to convulse with her orgasm, milking him of every last drop of cum. What seemed like hours but probably only seconds later, Rowan's body relaxed. Her limbs felt like jelly and they slipped from around Quinn to fall to the bed. He'd slumped on top of her, his breath hot and fast, bathed her neck. She couldn't raise more than a grunt when he spoke.

"Too heavy." Quinn levered up on his elbows but didn't get off.

His fingers swept the hair from her face. Cupping her jaw, he tipped her face up and placed a butterfly light kiss on her mouth. Rowan forced her eyelids open and found herself staring into Quinn's caramel brown eyes.

"It's so good to have you in this bed."

Rowan laughed.

"You know what I mean." He smiled and gave her another kiss. "But *having* you in this bed is pretty damn good too."

He rolled to the side and got off the bed. With his arms stretched over his head, Quinn's back and ass were on perfect display. She watched, mesmerized by the shift and flex of muscle and sinew under smooth tan skin. Licking her lips, she imagined running her tongue down his spine and dipping into the crack of his ass. Nibbling her way across the curve to the crease where leg met butt. He was one fine specimen of mankind standing naked for her enjoyment.

"If you're not careful you'll drool all over the bed," he said.

Slowly she brought her gaze up past his rear end, up the line of his back and to his face. He looked at her over his shoulder with a grin. Rowan smiled, not worried about getting caught ogling him.

"A little drool can't hurt. It's only water." He turned and gave her an eyeful. She swallowed. "Besides, I find my mouth suddenly dry."

Quinn threw back his head and laughed. The deep rumble shook his chest and made his cock bob. At half-mast, his erection stood out from his torso, the base was surrounded by dark hair and his large balls swung free below. She turned on her side and reached out to skim one finger from sac to tip and back again. Quinn shook and his cock grew harder. Palming the length, she gripped tight and pumped her hand up and down.

"Enough." He stepped back, pulling away. "You need rest." He scooped up the discarded sleep shirt and tossed it at her before stalking off to the bathroom, naked butt jiggling all the way.

Flopping back on the bed, she debated showering but gave up on the idea when the comfort of the bed proved too enticing.

The temperature in the room was warm in spite of the cold wind howling outside the window. The storm blowing up would likely dump snow overnight and turn the weather below freezing. But here in the comfort of the home she'd been born in she could rely on the furnace to do its job and keep the sub-zero temp at bay.

Listening to Quinn run the water in the bathroom, Rowan closed her eyes. The rattling pipes, the wind whistling under the eaves and the creaking of timber settling were a welcome reminder of everything this house meant to her. Comfort, safety, home.

QUINN WASHED UP QUICKLY. He grabbed a clean towel and washcloth and headed back to Rowan. She looked so peaceful lying sprawled on the bed and as he got closer her soft snoring reached his ears over the storm outside. Sound asleep and more beautiful than he remembered, she took his breath. To see her here, in their bed, the one he'd carved himself, made his heart whole for the first time in six years.

He sat on the edge of the bed, admiring the changes in her lithe body. She'd always been slim, but now that was tempered by sleek muscles and womanly curves. Her black hair was damp and plastered to her forehead, her face still flushed from their earlier exertion. Soot-colored eyelashes fanned over her cheeks and her pink lips, slightly parted, invited him to kiss.

Nothing else would please him more than to lean over and lick her pouty mouth but it was late already and they had so much to face in the next few days that he couldn't bring himself to disturb her slumber. He used the warm washcloth to clean her up, trying not to wake her. A few times she stirred but she remained asleep while he wiped and dried her. Wadding the cloth and towel together, he threw them in the general direc-tion of the bathroom.

Quinn folded back the bedding on one side and gently rolled Rowan over onto the sheet. Covering her with the quilt, he walked around the bed and climbed in on the other side. Putting an arm around her waist, he pulled her back until her spine nestled against his chest and her ass cradled his cock. The crease between her cheeks made the perfect resting place for his erection.

The wind howled outside as the storm picked up force. The legendary whistle that had given the mountains their name grew louder. Older members of the pack talked of the mountains whispering to those who chose to listen. It was a tale told for generations and even though Quinn didn't believe most of what was said, he knew from experience that once the moun-tain whispered it was best to find shelter. The predicted snow-fall was going to be a big one.

He pulled her body closer to his, her murmured protest reminding him not to squeeze the life out of her, but he could help it. He wanted to hold her and never let go. The next few days would be busy and if the snowstorm brewing dumped too much of the white stuff they'd be stuck at the house. There was no way he'd risk the mountain road if there was more than a foot of snow on the ground.

No doubt by now Marcus would have spread the word of Rowan's return. He wouldn't let an opportunity like that pass without using it. Quinn could only image what crap he'd make up this time. The man lived to cause trouble and did so every chance he got. But unlike in their youth, when Marcus's father was regal and later sovereign, he wouldn't be able to cover up any attempt he made to get at Rowan so easily.

Quinn would need to keep his wits about him too. He'd wanted nothing more than to squeeze the life out of Marcus for calling Rowan a bitch and if she hadn't been there he probably would have. Her steady calm had spread over him and kept him from doing something stupid and playing right into Marcus' hands. Before they went anywhere, they needed to sit down with Brogan and work out a strategy.

Without knowing what Marcus had planned, they wouldn't be able to do much in the way of prevention but they could certainly be prepared for the worst. Quinn didn't think Rowan would have difficulty being accepted back into the pack and the Council had been questioning Brogan on her possible return since the moment he became sovereign. They were more than ready for her to come home and take her place as royal.

He was being selfish but he wished there was a good dump of snow between now and morning. It would allow him to keep her to himself for a little longer. They had a lot of catching up to do. He wanted to know everything she'd done, everywhere she'd been. He wanted to tell her all that he and Brogan had done for the pack in her absence and he wanted to roll between the sheets until neither of them could stand.

Nuzzling the side of her neck, Quinn breathed in deep and sucked in a lungful of her scent. Wrapped in his arms, she was all he wanted and he'd do anything to protect her. If push came to shove, he'd take Marcus out and worry about the consequences later. Nothing and nobody would hurt her or force her to leave her home again. He cuddled into her back and let the comfort of having her here sink in. Rowan continued to snore softly and he let the warmth of holding her and the sound of the raging weather lull him to sleep.

QUINN JOLTED AWAKE, reaching for Rowan as he sat up. Already up and moving off the bed, she grabbed for a shirt.

"What the hell was that?"

He didn't get a chance to answer her, the door flung open and Brogan burst into the room. "Are you two all right?" He scanned the room for some perceived menace.

"We're fine. What was it?" Quinn asked while he pulled on pants.

"I think we've got a broken window. I thought it came from in here." Brogan turned and left as quickly as he'd come in.

"I think it was my old room," Rowan said as she followed her brother out the door, Quinn right on her heels.

Brogan stood three feet inside the doorway of Rowan's old room staring at the mess of broken glass and snow littering the floor and furniture. They hadn't left much in this room, a queen bed and dresser the only large items. There was a small writing desk and chair in one corner and a plush recliner in another. The desk and dresser remained unmarked but the bed and recliner had a layer of snow and glass glittering on them. The wind howled through the window and filled the room, dropping the temperature a good thirty degrees. Rowan shivered and Quinn moved around her to block the worst of the cold.

"How would the wind pick up a rock and hurl it through the window?"

"What rock?" Quinn surveyed the debris for what she was talking about.

Brogan stepped forward and Rowan's hand shot out and stopped him in his tracks.

"You've got no shoes on, Brogan."

Her reminder came just in time. They were all barefoot and not exactly dressed to tackle the clean up and repair of the window. Walking backward, Quinn pulled Rowan with him as he moved into the hall.

"Close the door to stop the chill from getting into the rest of the house, Brogan. We'll get dressed and clean this up now. I'm not leaving it until morning, if the snow gets any worse the room will be soaked by then." Rowan spun away from them and went back to their room.

"The weather didn't do this," Brogan said.

Quinn thought the same but remained quiet on the subject for now. "Let's fix the window first and worry about the rest later."

He found Rowan not getting dressed but standing by the window peering out into the darkness. The rollers on the timber door of the wardrobe squeaked as he pushed it open. He grabbed jeans and a flannel shirt to throw over his T-shirt. She hadn't moved when he turned back and he walked over to see what she was looking at.

"Why would someone be out on a snowmobile in near blizzard conditions?"

"What?" Quinn cupped his hand on the glass and scrutinized the darkness. "I can't see a damn thing."

"Over by the trees on the left, see the tracks? They're not covered because of the tree canopy."

She was right. Once he knew where to look, his keen coyote vision picked up the distinct trails of a snowmobile leading off into the forest. It appeared he'd be going out in the storm to scout around. He wouldn't follow the path cut into the snow but he'd be sure to find anything that might have been left behind. If the person had sat watching the house for long there could be a clue as to their identity. Not that he needed one. His gut told him it was Marcus but what was he playing at throwing rocks?

Quinn was of the opinion the man was impulsive and stupid but sitting in a snowstorm in the dead of winter was downright insane. And if Marcus had crossed over that fine line into the mentally unstable they were in for far more trouble than he ever could have imagined or expected.

10

"YOU ARE NOT GOING out there in this weather. I don't care who was skulking around the house, I'm not letting you put yourself in danger when the culprit is long gone," Rowan yelled at him.

She'd been yelling at him since he'd told Brogan he'd go out and take a look around while they secured the window and cleaned up. He understood her concern but it was misplaced, there would be no taking chances with the storm and darkness awaiting him. Quinn wanted to catch the person but he wouldn't risk his own neck to do it.

"Stop yelling at him, Rowan. He's doing his job and you know it. The quicker he's out there, the quicker he's back." Brogan thrust hammer and nails into her hands. "You can watch from the damn window if you want."

It was a wonder Brogan didn't crumple to the floor with the look his sister gave him. Before she could open her mouth and start yelling again Quinn tried to reassure her he'd be safe and calm her down. That temper of hers was mixing with her stubborn streak and he didn't want any more mess to clean up tonight. He remembered the arguments the siblings used to have. Nothing was safe unless it was nailed down, which worried him more now that Brogan had given her the timber and steel tool.

"I'm going to walk around the house and then out to the tree line, no farther. I promise." He planted a kiss on her lips and scooted out the front door before she could stop him.

Snow slapped his face and the wind cut through the layers of clothes he wore. The weather had eased up a little but there was already a good ten inches of ground cover. Slowly he combed the area around the house, the snowfall had covered any evidence of an intruder but then they might not have gotten that close. The rock could have been lobbed from a fair distance, if the thrower had a good arm, and he recalled Marcus being a damn good baseball player in their youth, the star of their high school team.

Quinn headed over to the tree line, his boots sinking into the drifts of snow. It made for slow going and with the wind threatening to blow him away he struggled to stay on his feet. The area between the house and trees yielded no more than his initial search. Quinn could see where the machine had been parked. A trough beneath a tree about six feet in gave it away. He examined the immediate vicinity, coming up empty. Frustrated, he sighed and looked up, color catching his gaze.

Caught in a low branch were strips of fabric. Standing still, he studied the small pieces of material. They were ripped from a snow jacket, a black and red one. He stepped over to get a better look. On closer inspection, Quinn determined they were from the sleeve of a well-worn parka. He had one very similar in his closet. Anyone who'd attended Whispering Springs High School had one. There were no distinct markings, so unless they could locate the rest of the coat, their chances of proving who was out here were nil.

Irritated at yet another dead end, Quinn made his way back inside. The wind had died down making the slog across the yard easier. As he rounded the corner of the house the door flew open and Rowan stood there waiting for him. It certainly beat any welcome he'd ever received from Brogan. Stomping the snow from his boots on each step, he took his time. He wanted to savor this homecoming. The first of many ahead in the future but this one would always be special. He cleared the threshold and stepped into the welcoming warmth.

Rowan closed the door and latched the deadbolts behind him. He stumbled back into the wall when she launched into his arms, her lips landing on his. It took a moment for him to act but once his brain engaged he swept his tongue into her mouth. In an instant he went from cold to hot. Her flavor seeped into him, spread out and teased his senses until all he could think of —could feel—was Rowan. She took over, turned his thoughts to one thing only. Getting naked and claiming her.

"Ahem."

Quinn untangled their tongues and pulled free. Dazed, they stared at each other, breathing hard.

"When you two are ready, I'll be in the living room." Brogan's footfalls echoed in the foyer.

"Damn." Quinn let her unwind her arms and lowered her to the floor, when he'd picked her up he hadn't a clue. "Hold that thought, we'll get back to it after I tell you both what I found."

Rowan nodded and reached for his hand. Fingers curled together they went to join Brogan. Someone had stoked the fire and Quinn unzipped his jacket and draped it over the back of a chair to dry. He shucked his boots and placed them on the hearth before he sat on the floor so his soaked jeans didn't wet the sofa.

"Well? Did you find anything?"

Quinn smiled at Rowan's impatience. He was surprised she'd waited this long before grilling him for information.

"Nothing other than you're right, there was someone out there. They were in the tree line for a while but I couldn't tell if they'd gotten close to the house or not. Too much snow."

"So do you have a theory?" Brogan asked.

"Yeah. They were in the trees watching the house for a long time. The depression from the snowmobile was still there. I found part of a jacket sleeve caught in a low branch, whether it happened before the rock was thrown or after, I can't say. But what I can say is there's no way to prove who did it. The material is from a Whispering Springs High parka, could have been anyone."

"But you think it was someone," Brogan stated.

"Marcus." Rowan spoke before Quinn could voice his thoughts.

He turned to stare at her. "Why would you think that?"

"Because the rock was thrown into my old room. It's not the first time he's tossed rocks at that window. Only last time they were pebbles and he only wanted my attention, not to hurt me." She shrugged. "That didn't come until later."

"Why don't I know about this? You've never mentioned him doing that." Brogan's words rang with shock at this new revelation.

"Mom and Dad knew. It was when I was about thirteen I think. He only did it a couple of times and then stopped. I don't know if Dad said something to him or if he got the hint that I wasn't interested."

One more reason for Quinn to hate the man, not that he needed more than Marcus' attack on Rowan as grounds for hatred. His jaw clamped and he ground his teeth together at the memory of her coming home bruised and bleeding. If she hadn't begged him not to leave her he would have gone out and hunted Marcus down that night. Brogan had stopped him from going after the bastard when they'd gotten her off the mountain, but he could still feel the boiling anger, still taste the need to kill.

"Quinn?"

He turned to Rowan, saw the concern on her face and cursed himself for not being able to hide his feelings. She had enough to worry about without him adding to the pile, he needed to remember that. One way to take her mind, and his, off things was to lose themselves in each other. In a few hours it would be daylight and they would have to think about the outside world but for now he'd make sure the only thing she thought about was him and the mind numbing pleasure he gave.

ROWAN WATCHED the emotions flicker across Quinn's face. He went from pissed off to aroused in record time. The sad part, or maybe it was a good thing, she found every one of his expressions appealing. He turned her on just by breathing but when he really set out to push her hot buttons he proved lethal. And if she was any judge, Quinn had decided it was time for bed.

He got to his feet and stalked toward her. Wrapping a hand around her upper arm, he hauled her off the sofa to her feet and marched her out of the room.

"Yep. No worries. See you both in the morning." Brogan's words and laughter followed them into the hall.

"Quinn?"

He ignored her. This take-charge man all but dragging her

to his cave had her blood pumping and her juices flowing. Why was she so ready to submit to his forceful nature when it came to sex? In everything else she challenged him but in this she turned into a swooning female eager to surrender to his command. A shudder moved over her. Her breasts grew heavy and her nipples puckered tight. The ache in her clit pounded in time with her galloping heart.

The toe of her sneaker caught the edge of a step, her knee missed the tread by a hair when Quinn picked her up and tossed her over his shoulder in a fireman's hold. Her head bounced and bumped into his back. Rowan wound her arms around his middle and hugged his spine. He took the rest of the stairs two at a time and slammed the door closed with his foot as he entered their room. Wasting no time, he dropped her on the bed and came down on top of her.

His mouth took hers in a hungry kiss. He thrust his tongue inside, savagely taking hers prisoner and delivering a delightful blend of give and take. Hands fumbled with clothing, each attempting to remove whatever fabric was within their grasp. Limbs tangled and frustration mounted. The desire for skin on skin slashed with a razor's edge, tearing at nerves with wicked need.

Their lips separated, breaths mingling as they gasped for air in the vacuum of sexual demand. Trapped by Quinn's burning gaze, Rowan stared at hunger so great she feared being devoured whole. Answering want filled her, clawed at her insides and stirred her coyote. The snarl and snap of a beast greedy for its mate echoed in her soul. Quinn's caramel eyes turned yellow as his coyote answered the call from hers.

A growl rumbled in his chest and vibrated up his throat, the sound muffled by his clenched jaw. Natural instinct had her whimpering and exposing her neck, offering herself to him. His nostrils flared and he bent down to lick the vulnerable column.

With gentle laps, he bathed her tender skin. He kissed and nibbled his way to the sensitive hollow beneath her ear. Tickled and teased until she squirmed beneath him.

The frenzied need abated. Her surrender to him soothed the raw need to claim. Now the urge was to savor, enjoy the spoils of the gift given. Slow, deliberate moves weaved their spell and turned her body pliant under his fingertips. He removed her clothing piece by piece, exploring each inch of skin revealed. Lulled into a sexual stupor, Rowan wallowed in the bliss flowing through her.

His magic hands and mouth worshiped her, made her world a kaleidoscope of heavenly pleasures. When he parted her legs to delve between her folds, Rowan arched off the bed, sensation saturating senses and mind. The peak came quickly and took her by surprise. Hurtling over the edge, she clawed his scalp as she held on to the center of her universe.

As her orgasm ebbed he rose above her, stripped off the remainder of his clothes and covered her body with his. Skin on skin from chest to knees, lean muscle met willowy curves. Her spread thighs cradled his hips and his cock pressed on her engorged pussy, hurling electric jolts of want into her womb. Coated in her cream, Quinn slid his erection back and forth, probing her entrance before moving back to bump her clit. He reached for her hands, held them beside her head and entwined their fingers.

Eyes locked on his, Rowan saw love and lust swirl together in a potent mix of longing. Holding her gaze, he lowered his face and sealed his mouth to hers. The kiss soft—gentle. He flexed his hips and lined his shaft up with her opening. His girth stretched her as he entered. With a long drawn out thrust, Quinn drove home, filling her completely. Her groan of relief was swallowed by his hungry lips. His tongue caressed her mouth the way his length stroked her pussy.

A slow, easy rhythm took them up the path to satisfaction. Each pass of his cock a carnal glide on their ride to heaven. Every brush of his tongue a slick lash of sinful delight. Lured into his world of leisurely passions, Rowan followed where he led. Seduced and tantalized by Quinn's languid movements, she relished the sensation of total abandonment of control. Fingers curled in his, she held on as he took them higher into the bliss of promised ecstasy.

When her climax broke, it swept her up and flung her to the winds. The shattering of body and mind so absolute she felt nothing but the man above her, driving into her faster. Harder. One final lunge and Quinn jerked before he buried himself to the hilt and stayed there. Warmth bathed her core as his cum spilled inside her. Fingers and toes tingled, arms and legs heavy as lead weights, Rowan sank into the mattress.

Quinn shifted to the side, his cock slipped free and her walls clenched in regret. Flutters traveled the length of her channel to her womb, squeezed her tummy tight. Breath after breath rasped in her ears, accompanied by the beating of her heart. Blood rushed in her veins, the echoes of lust tainting the flow. Drained of energy, she let her eyelids close and floated off to sleep.

BY THE TIME Quinn found the strength to move Rowan was asleep. On her back, arms and legs sprawled, she looked dead to the world. Sweat stuck her bangs to the side of her face and he smoothed them back with his fingers. Her rosy cheeks had a sheen of moisture and her scent drifted in the air to tease him. She looked so peaceful in her slumber, he tried to shake the bed as little as possible when he climbed out and headed for the bathroom.

Business taken care of, he washed up and went back to bed.

Lying next to Rowan, he pulled the covers up and tucked them both in. Predawn light could be seen through the window and Quinn glanced at the clock. Less than two hours until sun-up. Today would be a long one. Flakes still fell from the sky but the wind had slowed to a breeze. If it stopped snowing soon they'd be able to head into town after lunch.

He heard Brogan moving around downstairs and figured his friend had decided not to bother going back to bed. If it wasn't for the warm woman sharing his bed, Quinn would be staying up too. But he'd rather be awake next to a sleeping Rowan than wandering the house in the early hours of the morning. Turning on his side, he lifted the blanket and watched Rowan's breasts rise and fall with each breath.

Her creamy skin, marked in places from his teeth and beard stubble, tempted him to taste. Large nipples stood at attention like soldiers guarding a fort. He ran a finger around one pouty tip, it puckered into a tight little bead and the normally pink flesh darkened. She stirred, snorted a choked breath and turned over presenting him with her back. The notches of her spine protruding in a long line of follow the dots.

Resisting the urge to trace the delicate row of bones, Quinn moved closer and spooned his body around hers, gratified when she snuggled back against him. He slid one arm beneath her and cupped her breast with his hand. The other, he draped over her side and splayed his fingers across her stomach. Her ass nestled into his groin, his cock slipping snug between her cheeks.

He'd had more sex in the last twenty-four hours than he'd had in his entire life. He should be exhausted and totally sated but he still had a hard-on and his coyote would be more than happy to claim his mate again. The need no longer held the raw edge of starvation, the long abstinence satisfied by the feast of the last day. He burrowed his nose into the hair at her nape, breathed deeply and filled his lungs with her scent.

The house creaked around them and the wind rattled the windowpanes. Rowan continued to sleep, her soft snore and even breathing something Quinn cherished. For the second night in a row she slept in his arms. The reality far better than any dream he'd ever had in the years without her. Until yesterday he'd been clueless to the joy of holding her through the night. When she'd staggered into the house that fateful night long ago neither of them knew there were only hours left before circumstances would tear them apart.

He suppressed a shudder as the memory of Rowan's bloody and bruised body collapsing on the kitchen floor flashed in his mind. By the time he and Brogan had managed to tend to her wounds she'd roused enough to tell them what happened to her. Quinn's blood ran cold even thinking about what she'd survived at the hands of Marcus. It soon boiled when he imagined getting hold of the asshole and ripping him to pieces. One small bit at a time.

Quinn's wandering mind strained more than his heart. Muscles tensed and ready to fight squeezed hard, involuntarily, banding around her like a straight jacket. Rowan squirmed in his embrace, squeaked a protest. She settled quickly once he loosened his hold. He waited for her breathing to even out again and then gradually worked her out of his arms. Turning to his back, he stared at the ceiling. Deep breaths and the knowledge she lay beside him unharmed helped to rein in his anger.

Calm, Quinn gave up on sleep and slipped from the bed. Careful to make no noise, he grabbed some sweats and a shirt from the dresser. He dressed and checked she was covered up before he left the room and headed downstairs. None of the chill remained from the broken window and he descended the stairs in sockless feet. The smell of fresh coffee pulled him in the direction of the kitchen. Brogan sat at the island bench, a steaming mug clasped in his hands. Quinn helped himself to a cup of the dark liquid.

A sip to test the temperature preceded a mouthful of the rich wake-me-up elixir. Strong and black, just the way he liked it. The stool legs scraped when he pulled out the seat opposite Brogan. They sat in silence, sipped at their cups of caffeine and waited for dawn to arrive. Light came flooding in through the big glass windows in the back wall and as the sun rose to blanket the mountains, the blue sky showed its cloud-free expanse.

"How is she?"

Quinn didn't answer Brogan's question right away. He thought about Rowan and how she'd dealt with the obstacles so far. Her biggest freak-out moment had come when he'd gone out to investigate their rock thrower.

"She's ready."

"Good. We'll need her to be."

Quinn raised a brow. "Oh?"

Brogan shrugged. "A gut feeling." He sipped his coffee. "I think Marcus has gone over the edge. The rock was juvenile and not something a focused man would do. An obsessed one, yes, but one who's rational and methodical would never use such immature tactics."

He had to agree with Brogan's assessment. At some point Marcus had crossed a line. Quinn only hoped it wasn't Rowan's return that made him snap but knew it was a fruitless wish. With the pack's royal now back, Brogan's position as sovereign strengthened and so did Quinn's as regal. There had never really been a threat to their appointed status, but the trouble Marcus caused while they guided the pack made it harder to move forward and cement all their futures.

If he let himself be honest he'd have to admit the only sure way to see the pack prosper for generations to come would be to remove Marcus. The council would never vote to exile any pack member without a valid reason and hard evidence to back it up.

Until Marcus slipped up they were stuck with him.

11

ROWAN WOKE to bright sunshine and an empty bed. Curled under the quilt, she took her time stretching the kinks of sleep from her body. A glimpse of the clock told her it was well past time to get up. Muffled noises from below could be heard over the twitter of a bird outside the window. She rolled over and stretched her arms above her head, arched her back and popped bones stiff from slumber.

Sleep encrusted eyes squinted at the blaze of light through the open blind. She had to remember to close that before going to bed tonight. Mornings weren't her favorite time of the day. She'd go so far as saying she hated them and with her usual reluctance she threw back the covers and crawled out of bed. Her fists scrubbed at her eyelids as she made her way to the bathroom to attend to the need suddenly making its presence known low in her belly.

The house may have been kept a comfortable temperature but the warmth hadn't extended as far as the toilet seat. The shock of cold to her ass and thighs sucked the breath from her lungs. She couldn't get done quick enough and shivered from top to toe while her bladder emptied out. Finished, she debated a shower but decided to find out where Quinn was first. Walking through the bedroom, she picked up last night's clothes a piece at a time, like a treasure hunt she collected articles and threw them on.

Her teeth felt furry and she was sure to have morning breath but before she could return to the bathroom to fix either the smell of coffee filtered into the room. Closely followed by Quinn. She growled and lunged for the mug in his hand. He handed it over readily and she gulped down the lukewarm contents, the strong, dark blend well on its way to improving her day.

Quinn's chuckle skipped over her nerves and danced down her spine. He leaned in to place a kiss on her nose. "You're cute all sleep rumpled and grumpy."

"Grumpy? Who's grumpy? I'm too brain dead to manage grumpy yet."

He took the empty cup from her and, gripping her shoulder in one large hand, turned her toward the bathroom. A little nudge and he pushed her a step away. "Go get showered, you need to get ready to face the day."

About to protest about getting another coffee, it wasn't words that left her mouth. With a yelp, she jumped when Quinn slapped her ass to get her moving. Peering over her shoulder with narrowed eyes, she mumbled about rough treatment and missed coffee but did as he'd suggested and went to take a shower. His laughter echoed around the room. The only thing stopping her from smacking him back was his promise of more coffee when she was done.

Rowan kept her shower short. The enticement of fresh brewed coffee and a rumbling stomach too much to ignore. Wrapped in a towel, she went in search of clean clothes. The dresser produced underwear and T-shirts; in the wardrobe she found jeans and jackets. Everything she'd sent home with Brogan had been laundered and put away. Either someone came in and cleaned house for her brother and Quinn or they'd become very domesticated over the years. She imaged the two alpha males in aprons and gloves scrubbing bathrooms and mopping floors.

Laughing, she left the room and went downstairs. Her sock covered feet made no sound as she descended the stairs and followed her nose to the kitchen. The deep tones of Quinn's voice could be heard through the door and Rowan's nerves did a little happy dance in response. But the second she pushed the door open every part of her centered on the coffee pot in the corner. Zeroing in on the machine, she grabbed a cup off the counter and was sipping on liquid good-morning in seconds. Eyes closed, she savored the hot brew.

"I see you've grown to love mornings, Rowan." Brogan's voice spoke in her ear just before he kissed the top of her head.

Opening her eyes, she met his gaze, his laughing, hers narrowed with mock anger. "Aren't we the jokester this morning?"

Quinn chuckled. "Told you she was the same sunny Rowan."

"Humph." She turned back to refill her mug and ignored both of them.

Brogan ruffled her damp hair like he used to do when they were younger. Emotion choked her. Tears stung her eyes and clogged her throat. She sucked in a breath, chewed on her bottom lip and willed the tears away. Concentrating on the view out the window, Rowan swallowed past the lump in her throat. A couple of deep breaths and she was under control again, the urge to bawl her eyes out gone.

With a smile on her face, she turned away from the window. Mug full of coffee, Rowan walked over and pulled out a stool. Perched on the seat, she watched as her brother went back to cooking bacon and Quinn popped bread into the toaster. They worked together efficiently to get breakfast on the table. It didn't take long before she found herself with a plate load of bacon, scrambled eggs and toast.

Timber scraped on tile as Quinn and Brogan sat down next to her. Stomach rumbling, Rowan forked up a mouthful of eggs. Flavor exploded on her tongue. Cheese, egg, garlic and onion combined in a fluffy delicious mixture of breakfast heaven. Her tummy gurgled in delight as the first bite hit. Another scoop and her taste buds tingled. Suddenly ravenous, she couldn't shovel it in fast enough. The crispy bacon soon followed the eggs. With her plate scraped clean, she pushed it away.

Washing the wonderful meal down with some coffee, Rowan looked up to find both men staring at her.

"What?"

Neither of them said a word.

"Well, what?" This silence was a little unnerving. She felt like a bug under a microscope.

"Do you want more?" Quinn asked, pushing his still full plate toward her.

"No. I want to talk about what's going on today." Rowan pushed back from the counter. "But first I want a refill."

Mug in hand, she headed for the pot and topped off her cup with the last of the strong blend. "That's the last of it. Should I make another pot?"

"I'm fine." Brogan held up his hand.

"I'll pass and you should slow down too. What's that? Your fourth?" Quinn asked.

"I wasn't keeping count but I can tell you I'm nowhere near my limit yet."

Rowan sat back down, warm mug cradled between her

hands and started the conversation she knew they had to have. "So, when are we going into town?"

"We're not. William called this morning. He'll be coming out to see us after lunch," Brogan informed her.

"Why would he do that?"

"Because he agrees with us that you shouldn't meet the rest of the pack yet," Quinn said. "And he'd like to talk to you away from everyone else first."

"Oh." Rowan could guess what William would ask her about. She wasn't sure if she was up to talking about why she'd left but ready or not the time had come to tell all.

"In the meantime I thought I'd take a walk in the forest and see if our late night visitor left any other clues to their identity. Want to come with me?" Quinn asked.

"Definitely." She gulped down the last of her coffee. "Just let me get some warmer clothes on and I'll be ready."

Rowan dumped her dirty dishes in the sink and rushed from the room. The thrill of getting out in the forest again energizing her more than the bucket-load of caffeine she'd consumed. Maybe they could shift and go for a run after they'd scouted around. Smiling, she charged up the stairs two at a time.

"DO you think it's wise to take her out with you?"

Brogan's question wasn't unexpected. Quinn had thought about taking her with him all morning but in the end he knew Rowan was more than ready to face her life here. He planned for them to share this life, and that meant the good and the bad.

"She'll be fine." He picked up his plate and took it to the sink. "I doubt she would let me go out without her anyway, and we both know I'm the best tracker out of the two of us so it would be me going out there." Dish rinsed and stacked in the sink, he went back to where Brogan sat.

"She does look better than the first time I saw her," Brogan said.

Reminded of how fragile she'd looked, Quinn frowned. "Yeah, she's always been tough, but watching her these last two days…" He shook his head. "Rowan has an inner strength that she hasn't even begun to tap into."

"Well let's hope she won't need to. But, knowing Marcus the way I do, I'm sure she will."

"Yes, but this time we'll be there to back her up."

Brogan stood. "Yes."

They cleared the rest of the dishes and loaded the dishwasher. With the kitchen spotless, they headed to the living room to wait for Rowan. Brogan stoked the fire while Quinn shoved his feet into his boots. The heat had done its job and dried his jacket since the wee hours of the morning. Lacing up his left shoe, he heard footsteps on the stairs and hastened to tie the right one. The crash that echoed from the hall had him on his feet and running from the room with Brogan on his heels.

Skidding to a halt, he stared at Rowan buried beneath a pile of boxes, shoes and jackets. The wide-open closet doors and her colorful choice of language revealed where the crash had come from. He'd been meaning to clear that cupboard out for months, looked like she'd done his job for him.

Quinn reached down and pulled her off the floor. She came up with a pair of boots, one in each hand. He recognized them; they normally sat on the top shelf out of the way. How had she managed to cause the avalanche when they'd been right in front?

"Damn. You pulled the whole shelf down, Rowan." Brogan had his head in the closet, inspecting the damage.

"If you didn't have all that junk up there it wouldn't have happened." Rowan pouted.

The look on her face made him laugh. He remembered her attempting to use that look on them when she was a teenager and needed to keep out of trouble. Some things hadn't changed at all. Quinn pulled her close and hugged her. Kissing the top of her head, he set her aside and helped Brogan put everything back in the cupboard. They'd go through it all later and throw out what they didn't need.

Behind him, Rowan pulled on her snow boots. He tossed a jacket at her, what she had on wouldn't keep the cold out for long. With the last shoe thrown back in, Quinn slammed the doors and hoped they all remembered to be careful next time they went in the closet. Brogan turned to him and slapped him on the shoulder.

"Watch your backs. I've got a feeling we haven't seen the last of our midnight guest and I want you both prepared for anything."

"No worries. We'll stick to the tracks if they're still visible and head back in as soon as we lose the trail."

"Stop acting like a big brother and best friend and start thinking like a sovereign," Rowan said.

"As sovereign I should be going out there."

"No, you should be sending out your best tracker. You might think I'm not ready to be Quinn's backup but I'm all you've got right now and I am capable of defending myself if there's trouble."

Before Brogan could change his mind, Quinn ushered Rowan out the door. "I'm not expecting anyone to still be out there, Brogan. We'll be careful."

"Don't take unnecessary risks." Brogan turned to point at Rowan. "Especially you."

Rowan rolled her eyes and leaped off the porch. He gave

Brogan a reassuring smile and followed her. The snow level hadn't risen since he was out here earlier. With any luck the snowmobile tracks would be nice and clear. As she lead the way across the yard, Quinn scanned the tree line to make sure he was right and there wasn't someone hanging around.

The sun had a bit of warmth to it. Soft snow squished under his boots and by the end of the day a lot of what had fallen last night would have melted away. They stopped at the tree line. With daylight it proved easy to see the trench from the snowmobile and the strips of cloth flapping in the gentle breeze. Rowan walked over to where the fabric hung in the tree and examined it closely.

"It was ripped free when he was leaving."

"How can you tell that?"

"The branch it's snagged on is facing toward the house, if he brushed past on the way to throw the rock nothing would have caught."

Quinn stepped over and looked at what she was talking about. "You're right. So after throwing the rock our friendly visitor made a run for it but before that he sat here watching the house."

They both stood near the dent in the snow bank and turned to look at the house. Quinn crouched to where he thought he'd be if he were astride a snowmobile. He had a clear line of vision straight into Rowan's old room. In fact the view was so good he'd be able to see her if she were standing at the window.

"Fuck," he cursed under his breath.

"Come on. Let's see where these tracks go." She tugged on his sleeve.

He needed to punch something. The thought of someone watching her boiled his blood. His suspicion of who their spy was made it worse. Rowan entwined her fingers with his and pulled him hard to get him moving. Before they took two steps,

Quinn yanked her back into his arms. He buried his face in the side of her neck, breathed deep and held her tight. The comfort of holding her close and knowing she was safe eased his anger and focused his mind.

Twin grooves led them through the forest in the direction of the mountain road that led to Whispering Ridge. A thirty-minute trek had Quinn sweating and he turned to see how Rowan was doing. He needn't have worried. She'd proven herself more than fit in the last two days and this little stroll in the woods didn't bother her. When they reached the gravel road the trail stopped. Another set of tracks took up on the road. Someone had driven a four-wheel drive up here recently.

One that had been parked right where the snowmobile disappeared.

With no way of telling the type of vehicle or owner, they'd reached a dead end. Again. A game of cat and mouse was the last thing Quinn wanted to play but as usual Marcus led them on a merry chase. He sighed, turned back to head the way they'd come. Rowan stood off to the side, her face all scrunched up in concentration.

"What?"

"I'm not sure." She took a deep breath. "Can you smell that?"

Quinn sucked in a breath. Slowly. The air was scented with coyote. Not natural but shifter. Two different individuals. Neither of them familiar to him. And if he wasn't mistaken, newly turned. It didn't make any sense but he wasn't going to hang around to work it out.

"Let's go."

He grabbed Rowan's hand and started jogging. There was no time to waste; he wanted her back at the house, safe from possible danger. It was rare for new coyotes to show up in Whispering Springs, even rarer for a human to show up and be turned. Scenting two on the air couldn't be good news. Quinn pushed her in front of him, let her hand go as she took the hint and ran.

They could run the distance in less than half the time it took them to walk. He could hear Rowan's labored breath ahead of him. Her long legs ate up the ground and he had to stretch to keep up with her. It wasn't enough. About half a mile from the clearing, two coyotes came at them from the side. Quinn went down hard as one of them slammed into his ribs. He rolled, pushed to his feet and ran. Thankful to see Rowan hadn't stopped, he followed.

Flashes of red flickered through the trees in front of him and he knew Rowan was on her feet and running as hard as she could. A glimpse of gray to the right was the only warning before one of the animals crashed into his legs, taking him to the ground again. The second coyote landed on his back stopping him from somersaulting to his feet but the momentum took them tumbling over the snow. He used his legs and arms to lash out and stop teeth from connecting with flesh.

Two on one wasn't a fair fight but Quinn couldn't worry about that now. He had to get free of these two. His fist smashed into the side of a head, bones crunched and pain seared up his arm. A boot connected with ribs, a nauseating crack and yelp of pain followed. Given a reprieve, Quinn jumped to his feet and sprinted after Rowan. No longer able to see her, he used his ears to listen but couldn't hear anything over his own harsh breathing and pounding heart.

Leg muscles burned. Pushing hard, he leaped over a fallen log. Between the trees, he made out the clearing, a blaze of red streaking across the white snow. He cleared the tree line only to be tackled again. Pain sliced into his knee and hip when he crashed to the ground. Air exploded from his chest and he could do nothing but gasp in agony. Jaws snapped, tore at fabric and ripped at skin. Stunned, he curled up and protected his neck with his arms.

"Quinn!"

Rowan's scream echoed over the yard, the blood-curdling shriek froze the blood in his veins. Sheer terror lanced his heart. Were there more than two of them? Adrenalin and coyote kicked in. He struck out, hit flesh and bone and kept going. Blow after blow landed with a sickening thud, each one stronger than the last. Unable to shift with the two animals attacking him, he had no choice except to fight in human form but a partial shift would give him strength—teeth and claws to do more damage. To hold the half shift took skill and concentration but Quinn was determined to win and save Rowan.

Nothing short of death would stop him reaching her.

Protecting her.

12

HER LUNGS BURNED with each choppy breath. Her legs screamed in pain and the stitch in her side threatened to double her over but she kept running. Every second counted. The house was in sight now, so close, just across the clearing. Pounding feet and paws echoed behind her and she fought the urge to turn around. She couldn't waste the time. Getting to the house and Brogan could be their only hope.

Flesh and bone collided behind her. Rowan glanced over her shoulder and stumbled at the vision of human and animals rolling in the snow. The blows, grunts and snarls a strange musical note on the air. A yowl of pain and her insides went cold.

"Quinn!"

Forced to turn away and continue went against everything her coyote wanted to do. Her mate was in trouble and she needed to help him. But her human side knew the best way to do that was to get to the house. Get Brogan and a gun. Her legs pumped harder, her chest ached and her eyes filled with tears she refused to let free.

Brogan came through the door, rifle in hand, and raced to meet her. He grabbed her arm, shoved her behind his back and braced the gun on his shoulder. The loud boom ricocheted around them. Aimed into the air, the shot was meant as a warning but it did no good. Three bodies—one human, two coyote—continued to wrestle. Brogan fired again.

Nothing happened. Among the rustling and tearing of cloth Rowan could hear the groans and yelps of pain as teeth and claws and fists found their mark. Firing over their heads wouldn't do it, these animals were in a frenzy and they wouldn't stop unless someone or something stopped them. She yanked the weapon from Brogan's hands. Before he could turn around and stop her, she lined up the sight and fired.

No thought. No breath.

One shot.

Her aim was true and the bullet went dead center between the eyes of one coyote. He fell to the ground, pushed aside by the still fighting bodies. The second shot was harder. With only the two of them, the risk of hitting Quinn grew higher. Brogan stood beside her. His calm steady presence gave her the composed nerves to pull the trigger. This time her line was accurate but a twist of torsos as she squeezed her finger sent the slug into the coyote's shoulder and not the back of his head.

Yelping, he backed away from Quinn. The animal's head thrashed from side to side as he limped toward the tree line. Brogan stripped off his clothes, but the coyote sensed danger and bolted into the forest. Rowan sped across the distance to Quinn. He'd rolled to the side but didn't move to get up and she feared they'd been too late. She dropped to her knees and put the rifle within easy reach. The blur of fur and legs sailed past them.

Brogan was on the hunt.

Quinn moaned and Rowan breathed a sigh of relief. His

clothes were torn, the legs and arms suffering the worst damage. Blood from numerous scratches soaked the fabric but the amount wasn't life threatening. Gently she examined him for broken bones. Nothing stood out but he'd need an x-ray to determine if his ribs were cracked. His groan when she pressed on his side indicated they were at least bruised.

"I'm okay."

Rowan's heart skipped and a sigh of relief slipped from her throat. "Dammit, Quinn, you scared the life out of me." She stopped herself from hugging him for fear of hurting him.

"Just need to catch my breath."

Gasps of pain accompanied every shift of position. His injuries made his progress to sit slow and awkward. Rowan grabbed his shoulder to steady him when he swayed. As soon as he seemed stable she let go but didn't move away to check the coyote. She didn't need to, death would have been instantaneous.

"Nice shooting." Quinn tipped his head in the direction of the carcass.

"Not good enough to get two."

"You got him and I sliced through his neck before you fired. I doubt he'll get far."

"Even if he gets far, Brogan will catch him."

"Help me up."

"Do you think you should move yet?"

"Rowan, if I don't get my ass off this snow the damn thing will be frozen solid and any scratches I have will be the least of my worries."

"Oh."

She wrapped an arm around his waist and together they stumbled to their feet. Steady, Quinn pulled away and began to walk to the house. Rowan stayed close but his steps were measured and sure. When they got to Brogan's clothing she realized she'd left the rifle with the dead coyote.

"Damn. Wait here." She jogged back but before she picked up the gun Rowan checked the dead coyote. There were no familiar markings on the animal and she didn't recognize his scent, but then, she'd been away so long he could be a newcomer to the pack.

"He's not one of ours."

Quinn's voice startled her. "I told you to wait."

"I'm fine, besides we need to move the body closer to the house."

He used Brogan's pants to tie around the torso of the coyote. It made a crude rope but would do to drag the corpse to the house. Quinn moved with ease and other than the ripped jeans and jacket there was no evidence of his recent fight for life. His shifter genes worked quickly to repair the wounds inflicted and return his strength.

Together they made the slow trek across the snow. With the adrenaline wearing off, Rowan started to shiver. When they reached the back of the house her whole body shook and her teeth chattered.

"Get inside where it's warm." Quinn nudged her toward the door.

"No. I'm not cold. It's reaction. I've never killed anyone before."

Quinn pulled her against his chest and held her tight. "You did what you had to."

"I know but still it's not something I want to do again in a hurry."

"Thank you."

"For what?"

"Saving my life."

"I don't think it would have gotten to that point." Rowan's

stomach somersaulted thinking about what might have happened.

"Maybe not, but it would have been worse if you hadn't taken action."

"Brogan would have made the kill if I hadn't."

"Speaking of him, here he comes now." He loosened his hold. "Looks like he caught the other guy."

Rowan turned in Quinn's arms. Brogan strode toward them on two legs, the limp body of the coyote slung around his shoulders like a wet towel. It struck her as odd to see her brother stroll naked in such an easy manner. Before she'd lived outside of the pack she never would have thought about it but after spending several years with humans who hide themselves in public she felt the urge to turn away and give him privacy. She'd have to get used to seeing nude bodies again.

Hands wrapped around the animals legs, Brogan shrugged his shoulders and flipped the carcass over his head. It landed with a plop in the rapidly melting snow.

"He bled out before I got to him." Brogan bent to retrieve his pants from where Quinn dropped them. "I think you sliced through his jugular. The blood trail was thick and short."

"Rowan's shot was off because he pulled back when I clawed him."

"So, any idea how we have two newly turned coyotes wandering around in the mountains?" Brogan asked.

"No. I'm not familiar with the human scent either. They've never been in town," Quinn said.

"We need to get them in to Doc. She'll be able to do a DNA test to determine if they were turned by one of the pack." Brogan zipped his jacket before turning to Rowan. "I see you haven't lost your shooting skills."

"I haven't fired a gun since I left. Not sure if it's a good or bad thing I didn't need to think about what I was doing."

"Considering you saved Quinn, I'd say good." Brogan pulled her in for a quick hug. "Okay, let's get these loaded in the back of the truck."

"Hey, wait a second, you said she. Is Doc Monroe gone?"

"Gordie's taken over the practice. Doc and Mrs. Monroe are touring around in a RV he bought and did up."

Rowan turned to Quinn. "Gordie came back?" Excitement bubbled in her veins at the thought of seeing her childhood best friend again.

"Yep." Quinn tapped Rowan on the nose. "And as soon as we get these coyotes loaded I'll drive you to town to see her."

She refrained from jumping up and down like a toddler but there was no way to contain the smile that stretched across her face. Five years apart, Rowan and Gordie had struck up a close friendship during their teenage years. They'd gone through their first shift together, she as a maturing coyote and Gordie as a newly turned one. When Gordie's mate and unborn baby were killed in a car accident, she'd left Whispering Springs and not returned before Rowan had made her escape.

The last time she'd seen Gordie was eight years ago. After leaving for college the summer after the accident, Gordie had only come home for short visits and didn't see anyone but her family. Rowan had missed the closeness the two shared, and until El, she'd gone without a close female friend. Of course El knew nothing about Rowan's heritage so there were parts of herself she had never shared with anyone but Gordie. The idea of reconnecting their friendship thrilled Rowan and spurred her into action.

Between the three of them, they moved the coyotes around to the driveway. Brogan must have shoveled the snow while Rowan and Quinn were out in the forest because the packed gravel drive was cleared off ready to use. How he'd managed to do it all alone she couldn't say. Quinn had parked her small rental behind his truck so she dashed inside to get her keys while the men loaded the bodies in the truck bed.

As she rushed down the drive her foot slipped on a patch of ice. Arms flailing, Rowan skidded about ten feet before going down. Flat on her back, the air sucked from her lungs, she stared up at the blue sky and fought for breath. The crunch of running feet as they sloshed through the snow and gravel came from the opposite side of the vehicle to where she landed. Quinn's face popped into view.

"Are you all right?"

Unable to speak, she nodded.

"Then talk to me." Panic was written all over Quinn's face.

"Can't." Pain filled her chest. "Yet."

Color drained from his face and he reached for her.

"No," she panted. "Give me a minute."

Lying on the hard-packed drive, Rowan took her time catching her breath and cataloging the aches and pains now racking her from head to toe. Other than a few bruises, she'd missed out on serious injury. She rolled to her side and sat up. Quinn's arm slipped around her shoulders. With her breathing back to a normal rate, she looked around for the keys that were flung from her hand when she hit the ground.

"Did you see where the keys went?"

"No."

They both looked around but the keys were nowhere in sight. Getting to her feet, Rowan turned around slowly. She couldn't see any holes in the snow so they hadn't sunk beneath the surface. Confused by their disappearance, she tried to remember the exact sequence of her fall and the moment her grip on the keys was lost. She'd slid a few feet on her back and the keys had left her hand as she landed, which meant they had to be near Quinn's truck.

Rowan stepped the few feet with care, she didn't want to

risk losing her footing again. The obvious place would be under the truck. The four-wheel drive sat a good two feet off the ground. The keys could have easily flown beneath it. She got down on her knees to peer below the chassis. A quick glance revealed the keys but they weren't the only thing she found. Next to the front right-side tire sat a large puddle of liquid. She might not know that much about cars but any idiot would know that amount of oily fluid spelled trouble.

"Ah, Quinn?" She reached out and retrieved her keys.

"Yeah." He crouched down beside her.

"When did you last drive the truck?"

"The day you arrived. Why?"

"There's a pool of oil or something under there." She pointed to the front wheel. "Way too much for just a small leak."

Quinn dropped to his stomach and shimmied underneath the cab. Rowan bent down again and joined him. He dipped a fingertip into the mass and brought it to his nose. One sniff and he pulled his hand away to rub the slick goo between his fingertips before wiping the excess off with a clump of snow. The space didn't allow for Quinn to turn over but he twisted his neck and began poking at the undercarriage.

"Fuck."

The curse echoed in the confined area and Rowan watched him yank a section of hose to get a closer look.

"Brogan, get under here and look at this," Quinn yelled.

"What is it?" she asked.

"Someone cut the brake line. This puddle is brake fluid."

"What's wrong?" Brogan's face appeared on the opposite side of the car.

"Did you take the truck out while we were at the cabin?" Quinn asked.

"No, I haven't used it since I drove back here the day

Rowan arrived." Brogan maneuvered his way under to get a better look. "Is that the brake line?"

"Yep. Sliced clean through."

"No way it was an accident. The cut is too precise." Brogan examined the hose in Quinn's hand.

"Looks like our midnight visitor got closer to the house than we thought," Quinn said.

The cold began to seep into Rowan's clothes so she left the men to their inspection and wiggled her way out from under the truck. A glance at her watch showed it to be after midday and the grumble of her tummy told her well past lunchtime. She brushed the snow from her clothes and decided a change of outfit was needed before they drove in to see Gordie. Quinn stood up beside her and Brogan strode around the hood to join them.

"William is due to arrive any minute. I suggest we lock up the back of the truck to keep our cargo safe and head indoors to get warm and dry before he gets here," Brogan said.

"Rowan, you go on in. We'll clear up out here and be in when we're done." Quinn nudged her toward the house.

"I can help." She got the feeling he was trying to get rid of her but couldn't think why.

"It'll only take us a minute and there's nothing for you to do anyway so you might as well go in and get changed."

He gave her another push and having no further argument, she went. She walked slowly, hoping to catch any conversation they may have without her there but neither of them said a word before she reached the front steps and out of earshot. Rowan took her time but once she had the door open and a blast of warm air surrounded her, she slipped inside and forgot about eavesdropping.

• • •

QUINN WAITED until Rowan closed the door behind her. "I don't think Rowan's the target."

"What makes you say that?"

"The attack earlier and now the cut brake line." Quinn held up a hand to stop Brogan from objecting before he finished explaining. "I agree the rock through the window of her old room looks like she's the target but the other two incidents point to me. Neither of those coyotes went after her when they could have and the truck is mine."

Brogan remained quiet. Quinn knew he was right. Rowan's involvement was pure luck. Marcus had been planning his latest attempt to disrupt their positions in the pack for a while, the claim he made to the Council the first of his moves to destabilize his and Brogan's leadership. His senses told him Gordie would find Connelly genes when she looked at the two dead coyotes. Their scent had a faint trace of Marcus but Quinn couldn't be sure if the bastard had anything to do with turning them.

"You think Marcus is trying to get rid of you?"

"Yeah, with me out of the picture it would be easier to remove you as sovereign."

"He might think so but you aren't my only support in the pack."

"I don't think that matters. He's crossed a line somewhere and isn't thinking rationally, not that he ever really did but now the end goal is to be sovereign and he'll do whatever it takes to get it."

"William will be here soon. He's one of the few who understand the danger Marcus represents. We'll explain what's happened and then take the bodies to Doc."

"It would be good to have it on record with the whole council. Do you think William could call a meeting for this afternoon?" Quinn slammed the tailgate shut. "It might be a good idea to call one anyway so Rowan can make her presence known."

"Good idea. Let's get inside and change so we're ready to go right we speak to William." Brogan turned and headed toward the house.

Quinn clicked the canopy lid on the truck bed in place and checked it was locked before following his best friend. He continued to run the events of the last twenty-four hours through his mind. The more he thought about it the more he was sure Marcus was coming after him directly this time. In the past he'd only caused general mischief but for some reason the ante had been upped. He just hoped they could stop anyone else from getting hurt.

13

QUINN SAT in the front of Brogan's truck. The three of them were following William into Whispering Springs. After they'd explained everything the older man had insisted they take the strays to Doc's office right away. The men had moved the bodies from Quinn's truck to the back of William's before starting out. Rowan sat beside him, equal parts excitement and nervousness coming off her. He knew she was worried about fronting the council but the prospect of seeing Gordie again put a smile on her face.

Both women had changed over the years but he hoped they would be able to reestablish their close friendship. It would be good for Rowan to have someone to connect with in the pack. A lot of her friends had moved away from the mountains and only returned for brief visits. One more thing they needed to change, too many of the younger coyotes were leaving the pack to live among humans in the big cities. They were changing that slowly and in time they planned to build a tourist industry around the mountains the pack called home.

The plans were going well, but to make sure their secret

remained safe they were building a resort farther down the mountain. The humans who came to enjoy what Whispering Mountains offered should have no need to venture into the town. Brogan's vision for the pack's future would breathe new life into an old world. Hopefully in time, some of the younger generations would return to build their lives here. A couple, like Gordie, had already returned and more of the younger ones were talking of staying instead of leaving.

No one spoke, each of them lost in their own thoughts, but it wasn't an uncomfortable silence. Instead it comforted, having his mate and best friend with him made Quinn feel all was right with his world. But it was a false comfort and until they removed Marcus as a threat, he couldn't be complacent. He would need to be on alert, they all did. Dirty tricks were to be expected at every turn and now it would seem that Marcus had gone a step further. Nothing would stop him getting what he wanted. Not even murder.

Whispering Springs came into view and Rowan sucked in a breath. Quinn turned to find her eyes sparkling with tears. He reached for her hand and entwining their fingers, he brought it to his mouth and kissed her palm.

"Welcome home," he said.

"I've missed so much. There are new buildings every-where." Rowan sniffled between words.

"Not that many but a lot have had facelifts and last summer saw most of the pack out slapping new paint on anything that stood still long enough," Quinn joked.

"We took a big hit the winter before. Four bad blizzards in a row did major damage to most of the older buildings. While we rebuilt those, we spruced up the rest," Brogan added.

"And Doc got a state of the art clinic to work in." Quinn let go of her hand and wrapped his arm around her shoulders. "We're heading there first."

She snuggled into his side, her head resting on his chest. He caught Brogan's look of concern and tried to reassure him with a smile. Rowan would be fine. Coming home had to be an emotional roller coaster for her and she was bound to have some shaky moments.

William took the street leading to the back of the clinic. With any luck no one would see them unloading the dead coyotes and they could keep the strays a secret from the rest of the pack until they knew where they'd come from and why they were wandering around in the forest. Brogan pulled in behind William, the back door of the clinic opened and Gordie stepped out. She shook hands with the councilman as they got out of the truck, then she turned to greet them.

"Morning, Brogan, Quinn..." Her eyes widened and her mouth dropped open. "Rowan?"

"Hi Gordie." Rowan stepped around him.

"Oh my God. It really is you." Gordie leaped forward, enveloping Rowan in a hug.

Quinn gave them some privacy and went to help the others with the coyotes. He didn't like tears in Rowan's eyes.

Not even happy ones.

ROWAN HELD ON TIGHT. The familiar scent and feel of Gordie soaked in and welcomed her home a little bit more. Memories bombarded her. Times when things were simple and life stretched before her without a worry teased Rowan, her innocence and naïveté had cost her dearly. In one violent act, her world had been destroyed by someone she thought she could trust. She would not let it happen again.

"I can't believe you're here." Gordie's voice was choked with tears.

"It's me. And you have no idea how glad I am to see you." Rowan spoke over the lump in her throat.

They pulled apart. Rowan took in the woman Gordie had become. Other than the tears on her cheeks, she looked every bit the professional doctor. From her white coat, open to reveal the tailored slacks and cream blouse beneath, the stethoscope draped around her neck to dangle against her chest to the glasses perched on her nose, her attire screamed "trust me". The heavy snow boots on her feet the only contradiction but she even managed to make them look good.

"Gosh, Gordie, you're as beautiful as ever."

A light flush filled her friend's face. "Stop it. Have you looked in the mirror at all? You'd get a dead man's pulse racing."

"Speaking of dead men." Rowan turned to watch the men take the second coyote into the clinic. "Let's get inside so you can hear what happened."

The smile left Gordie's face and she wiped the moisture from her cheeks. "Come on, we can talk after this is over."

Arm in arm, they followed the men into the clinic. Rowan waited for Gordie to secure the door before they walked down the hall and into an examination room. She took in the tables, cupboards and equipment and realized they were standing in a morgue. The two coyotes were laid out on steel trolleys and Gordie flicked a switch on the wall beside them. Lights suspended above each table blazed to life, illuminating the bodies.

"So, what have we got?" Gordie slid into doctor mode. She scrubbed her hands and pulled on gloves before she moved toward the closest corpse.

"They're newly turned and not from around here," Quinn said.

Gordie's gaze lifted and met briefly with William's before she turned to face Quinn. "Where'd you find them?"

"I didn't. They found me. Tried their best to take me down but Rowan fired the single shot that killed that one." He indicated the coyote Gordie stood next to. "The other one took a bullet to the shoulder and a slice to the neck before running off. He bled out before Brogan got to him."

"Where was this?" Gordie began examining the animal in front of her.

"In the forest behind the house."

"Any strange behavior before they attacked?" She peeled back the coyote's lips to reveal his teeth.

"We didn't see them until they attacked."

Again, Gordie glanced at William. There was something going on and Rowan wanted to know what.

"Why do you two keep looking at each other like that? What aren't you telling us?" she asked.

William gave a slight nod and Gordie turned to Brogan. "These aren't the first coyotes to be found. Last month I found one beside the road up near Steve's place. He'd been hit by a car and left for dead. I called William, who met me here, but there wasn't anything I could do, his internal injuries were too great and he'd lost a lot of blood. He died on the operating table."

"Why wasn't I told about this?" Brogan looked to William.

"Because we still don't know where he came from or who turned him. I didn't want to start any unnecessary panic by informing the council," William explained.

"I would have kept your confidence, William." He turned back to Gordie. "Can you see if these two are connected to the other one?"

"Yes, I'll do a DNA profile but I'll tell you now I don't

expect to find any more than I did last time. I can pin down the genetic line but not the direct link."

"You know what line?" Quinn asked.

"Yes."

"Who?" Brogan spoke through gritted teeth.

"Connelly." William said.

"What?" Brogan roared. "I'll kill him."

"That's the exact reason I didn't tell you before now. We have no proof that Marcus is involved and until we have hard evidence our hands are tied. You know the council will never exile him unless there are irrefutable facts linking him to any of his crimes."

"Fuck!" Brogan paced, his frustration clear.

Rowan looked at Quinn, the tension thrumming in the room could be cut with one of Gordie's scalpels. Seconds passed without a word. Gordie broke the silence by moving over to the second coyote. She snapped on a new set of gloves and got to work examining the animal. Rowan stood out of the way and watched as hair, organs and tissue samples were taken for testing. Not being squeamish around blood had its advantages.

Quinn and Brogan were talking in hushed tones with William on the other side of the room. She wanted to know what they were discussing but the body being dissected reminded her she'd killed. She'd hunted before but in coyote form, and only small vermin. Even though she'd had no choice, she should have shot to maim, not kill. The deaths of these two strangers would stay with her for life and though she had to come to terms with it, she refused to feel guilty for saving Quinn.

Gordie moved with precision and skill, and Rowan stared in awe at her childhood friend. The age difference had never worried either of them. They'd clicked on a deeper level than most teenage friends except the strain Gordie had been under after the accident made it hard to keep the friendship together. Rowan had cherished any time spent with her but had known things would be harder once Gordie left for college. The brief visits had been few and far between and even then she hadn't gotten more than a glimpse of Gordie. Distance and time had eventually seen them drift apart.

Now, with them both back in Whispering Springs, they could reestablish their bond as mature adults. She couldn't wait to hear all about Gordie's time living among humans, not that she would have found it as hard as Rowan had at first. Gordie had the advantage of being born human, Rowan only had the stories her friend told her to go on when she'd left town. Without those, she was sure someone would have found out what she really was. She wanted to tell Gordie all about El and Australia. The places she'd been and people she'd met. After the meeting with the council she would invite Gordie over for dinner.

"It'll take a while for the results but as soon as I know something I'll ring you."

Gordie's words snapped Rowan out of her thoughts. The men had moved to stand around the table and were listening to Gordie talk about similarities between these coyotes and the one from last month. If someone was turning humans and leaving them to fend for themselves they had bigger problems than rocks through windows and cut brake lines. Those misdeeds could hurt someone but turning humans and abandoning them could hurt the entire pack.

"This is worse than rocks through windows and cut brake lines, isn't it?" Rowan couldn't help voice her concern.

Quinn walked over and cradled her jaw in his hand. "If this isn't an isolated case we definitely have a bigger problem. But we'll find out who's responsible and stop them. I promise." He bent down and brushed his lips across hers. "For now, it's time to go meet with the council."

Rowan noticed William had left and Brogan waited at the door for her and Quinn. "Will you still be here after I've met with the council, Gordie?"

"I'm here until five. Come back after your meeting and have coffee with me. I don't have anyone booked but I can't guarantee I won't get a walk in."

Rowan smiled. "That would be great. See you in a while." She led the way outside, the heavy silence behind her spoke of how serious their troubles were.

QUINN ADMIRED the way Rowan worked the room. She had each of the council members eating out of the palm of her hand and didn't even know it. With concise explanations, she told them why she'd left and stayed away for so long. Her honesty and lack of hesitation in answering any question they threw at her won their respect and convinced them she only did what was right for her safety.

There were still a couple of the older men who refused to believe Marcus would do such a thing but they accepted her recount of the events and overlooked his involvement. If Quinn didn't know better he'd say Marcus was a cat shifter, the bastard certainly had nine lives. He continued to get away with every horrible thing he did. Unless they caught him red-handed there was little hope of the council voting to exile him from the pack.

He and Brogan sat quietly while Rowan and the council talked. Once they accepted her return, William opened the meeting to discuss the recent events and the turned strays that had shown up. The meeting went from calm to chaotic in seconds. Everyone had their own opinion of who could be responsible and no one could agree on how to handle the situation. With things going nowhere fast, William told each person in the room to go home and think seriously about what would be the best way to deal with the problem.

Quinn, Brogan and Rowan waited as the council members filed out. William remained seated and Quinn suddenly realized how old he was. Their coyote genes allowed them to live longer than non-shifters but they still aged. William had to be around one hundred. He didn't look older than fifty by human standards, but the last few years of instability had taken their toll on a number of the elder pack members. He knew Doc had put Vincent on bed rest the other month because of exhaustion and with their quick-healing genes it was a worry.

"Brogan, you need to find out who's behind this and stop them." William shoved his chair back and stood. "I don't care how. I don't want to know how, but you and Quinn need to eliminate the problem. Now."

"Are you telling me to...?" Brogan didn't bother to continue. The look William gave him before leaving the room was enough.

"Did he just tell us to do whatever it takes?" Quinn asked.

"Yeah, I think so." Brogan looked as stunned as Quinn felt.

As sovereign and regal they were supposed to be beyond reproach. One step out of line and the council would remove them and vote in another coyote. He didn't think William would set them up for a fall but they still weren't sure where everyone's loyalties lay and couldn't risk putting themselves in the firing line. They would need to be careful and watch their backs to be sure they weren't being set up to fail. Not that he really thought William would do that to them.

Rowan had remained quiet but he could tell by the look on her face she had something to say. "Out with it. What are you thinking?"

"I don't think you should step out of line like William alluded. I know I don't have any recent experience with the pack or the council but I'm telling you both now, crossing the line would destroy everything you've done in the last few years."

"I have no intention of crossing the line, Rowan. I'm concerned that William would even suggest it. Either he knows more than he's saying or he's afraid we'll be exposed if humans continue to be turned," Brogan said.

"So what do we do? We could ask Doc what she thinks. She's been doing that genetic study of coyotes. She's bound to have a theory." Quinn slipped his arm around Rowan's waist and led her out of the room.

"We can grab some coffee from the diner and head over there now. She's expecting me anyway," Rowan said.

They left the lodge and walked along the footpath. It was a quiet afternoon, the snowfall the night before kept most people at home but those who were out stared as they went past. Rowan grew tenser with every step and he tried to comfort her by tucking her tighter to his side.

"It's okay. They'll stop once word gets out but for now it's a shock to see me." She shrugged. "I guess I'll be fodder for the town gossip for a while yet."

They reached the clinic just as it started to snow again. Light flurries fell from clouds that threatened a heavier fall. "Go in and sit with Doc while we go grab the coffee." He steered Rowan toward the door.

"Okay, but I don't think we should stay in town too long. Those clouds look ominous."

He waited until she was safely inside out of the cold and snow. Steve McKenna called out to Brogan and Quinn left the two of them talking to duck across the road to the diner. He just stepped off the curb when an engine roared and tires squealed.

A shout from behind came a second too late. He turned to jump clear but his boot slipped on a patch of ice and he couldn't get enough grip to move quickly. The screech of tires and the scent of burning rubber filled the air and Quinn knew that only a miracle would save him from being hit.

The vehicle clipped his thigh and spun him around as it lifted him into the air. The weightless motion of flying rolled his stomach. He landed with a thud, the impact jarred every bone and rattled his head. Pain lanced his chest and shoulder. His vision blurred as his mind whirled. Shouts faded into the background as the agony rolled over him. One voice stood out among the others and he tried to hold onto it but his body couldn't take anymore and he slipped into the blackness creeping in.

14

ROWAN AND GORDIE ran from the clinic at the first screech of tires. They burst through the door and onto the footpath in time to see Quinn be catapulted into the air as the old truck connected with his side.

"Quinn!"

Her stomach dropped to her toes and her heart lodged in her throat as she raced the short distance to his inert body. Ignoring the shouts of warning and squealing of tires, Rowan fell to her knees next to him. He was twisted in an awkward position but she didn't dare risk moving him yet. She reached out and placed her fingers on his neck, his pulse beat steady beneath his skin. Eyes closed, he remained motionless.

"Rowan, get out of the way." Brogan's shout barely heard over the engine roar, rubber skidding on pavement and yelling.

She glanced over her shoulder for Gordie. The car speeding down the road chilled her blood and froze her limbs. Staring in horror, she watched it draw closer. The man behind the wheel stared back, an evil smile on his face as he aimed the vehicle straight at them. A huge black SUV sped past her and headed for the truck. With a crunch of metal, the two cars collided in a bone rattling crash. Glass exploded and showered the road around them. Rowan ducked her head and covered Quinn's face with her body.

Rowan's ears rang. The creak and groan of metal coming to rest made a strange symphony with the tinkle of glass on concrete. Her hands stung like hundreds of pins were stabbed into the back of them. Carefully, she lowered them from around her head and brought them down to look at. Tiny slivers of glass peppered her skin and the arms of her jacket. So small they sparkled like fairy dust. Drops of blood began to form around some of the larger pieces.

Feet pounded across the ground, shoes crunched on debris as people began to move. Voices yelled for others to help and sirens could be heard coming closer. Mercifully the snow had stopped falling at some point but it wouldn't be long before it started again.

Brogan scrambled over to her side. "Are you okay?"

"I think so. But Quinn hasn't woken yet. Where's Gordie?"

"Checking on the drivers." He looked past her at the mangled wreckage. "Steve's all right, he's climbing out now but the other guy doesn't look good. His head is at a weird angle."

"Steve was driving?" Rowan cleared an area next to Quinn and sat.

"He used his truck to stop the other guy from mowing you both down."

"Not soon enough for Quinn."

"How is he?" Gordie crouched down and started to check for injuries.

"He hasn't come to at all." Rowan brushed some hair from his face.

"God, Rowan, let me see those hands."

"They're okay, a few scratches, some glass still imbedded but nothing life threatening. Tend to Quinn first."

"We need to get him inside. Brogan, can you go in and get the spinal board? It's in the first exam room."

"Sure, did you check Steve?"

"Yeah, just bruising, the airbag saved him from serious injury."

"And the other driver?" Brogan asked.

Gordie shook her head.

"Another stray?"

"No. William and Steve are getting the area cleared so we can remove him from the truck and get him into the clinic as quickly as possible. As soon as we get Quinn inside I can deal with the other problem."

Rowan turned to see the crowd gathered on the street. A number of them pointed at the crashed vehicles and the dead driver. Steve removed a rug from the back of his SUV and used it to cover the body. Recognition struck her and she sucked in a breath.

"Malcolm Connelly."

"What?" Brogan asked.

"The driver. It's Malcolm Connelly."

"It can't be. He's been dead for two years."

"Brogan, go get the spine board. We need to get Quinn inside and Connelly out of sight before anyone else works out who the dead man is." Gordie felt down each of Quinn's legs without moving him. She looked up at Brogan who stood there with his mouth open. "Go."

Brogan spun and sprinted to the clinic. He returned in no time, the board under one arm. He placed it on the ground next to Quinn before going to talk to William. Steve came to help Gordie get Quinn ready. He stirred when they wrapped the collar around his neck to immobilize his head but he didn't come around until they lifted him.

"Fuck." The curse came out strained.

"Easy, big guy," Steve said.

"Don't call me names, shrimp."

Relief filled her. Quinn's injuries couldn't be too serious if he could joke with Steve. The three of them rolled him onto the spine board and Gordie secured the straps.

"I don't need this stupid thing." Quinn tugged on the bindings. "I took a bump to the shoulder, that's all."

"Then why were you out cold for so long?" Gordie asked.

"Sleeping on the job, big guy?" Steve pulled the straps tighter.

"Hey, not so tight, I'm not going anywhere."

Gordie reached for Rowan's hands and began picking out some of the larger pieces of glass. Blood welled up to bead on her skin and each tug was followed by a mild sting. Rowan breathed deep and tried not to focus on what Gordie was doing.

"I'll need tweezers for the rest." Gordie turned to Steve. "And you'll let me look at you when I've seen to Quinn and Rowan."

"Sure, Doc, you can touch me all you want." He grinned in an exaggerated leer.

Gordie gave him a dirty look and got to her feet. Steve watched her walk away, naked yearning in his eyes. Rowan didn't know what was going on between them and wouldn't ask but she'd have to remember to question Quinn later.

"Ready to go?" Brogan stepped over, Gordie and William close behind him.

"What's going on over there?" Quinn asked.

"Nothing you can help with at the moment." Brogan

gripped one end of the stretcher while Steve grabbed the other. "Let's get you inside and I'll tell you everything you missed."

"I can walk, you know. I'm not an invalid," Quinn grumbled.

"Just lie there and behave. I'm getting tired of seeing you on the wrong end of trouble, Quinn MacClellan," Rowan said.

"Yeah, listen to your mate or we might drop you on your head," Steve said. "Oh wait. You did get dropped on your head."

"Ha ha, very funny."

Rowan laughed at Quinn. He looked hilarious strapped to the stretcher with the sullen look on his face. The banter between him and Steve had dissolved most of her tension. As soon as Gordie told her Quinn was fine, the rest of her anxiety would be gone too.

QUINN LET Doc poke and prod and he allowed her to take x-rays, the whole time keeping quiet. He knew what she'd find. His head was hard as rock and there was no permanent damage from the whack it took. The other injuries were minor as well. He jarred his shoulder and landed on his already bruised ribs but with Rowan hovering over him every step of the way he let Doc do what she had to.

He refused the painkillers she offered. The fall had made his mind fuzzy enough. His shoulder would be stiff and sore, but already his ribs felt better. By morning he'd be good as new. Nothing beat coyote genes when it came to healing. Finally finished, they made their way to the room where Brogan, Steve and William waited with the corpse of the madman who'd tried to run him down. He needed to thank Steve for stopping the second attempt on his life.

Quinn walked into the room and stopped dead.

"Fuck. Is that who I think it is?" Had the bump on his head damaged his vision?

"Yes. Malcolm Connelly," Brogan said.

"Shit. I thought he was dead."

"So did the rest of us," William added.

"Christ. Dead man walking."

"We're trying to piece things together. But I think we've found our mystery turner of humans," Brogan said.

"I'll need to match the DNA samples but it's likely you're right." Doc went to the sink, scrubbed her hands and snapped on a pair of latex gloves.

"Where the hell has he been all this time?" Quinn didn't think anyone would be able to answer but he asked anyway.

"Maybe Marcus can help us out with the answer to that." Rowan stepped up beside him. "Why did you all think he was dead?"

Quinn looked at Brogan. There were so many things Rowan had yet to learn and he wasn't sure what Brogan wanted her to know. The fighting between pack members had lasted for years. When Brogan won the fight against Malcolm and the older man had fallen into the Canyon, everyone had assumed he'd died. Odds were Marcus not only knew his father was alive, but he'd been harboring him all these years.

"There's a lot you need to know but now isn't the time or the place. Any objections to me taking Quinn and Rowan home now, Doc?"

"No, but keep an eye on Quinn. I didn't see any hemorrhaging on the scan but you can never be too careful."

"I'll be fine. Let's go before the storm hits full force."

"There's not much we can do with the storm coming. Best if everyone gets home safe and sound and we'll meet as soon as the weather allows," William said.

"William, I want the council informed of Malcolm's

sudden appearance and I want it made clear that Marcus is a threat until proven otherwise."

"I'll go and ring everyone now. Not sure it'll get us what we want but at least he'll be watched more closely."

"I'll stay and help Doc clean up and secure the body. You guys get on home," Steve offered.

"Thanks, Steve. If you hear anything on the gossip line, let me know." Brogan fished his keys from his pocket.

Quinn slid his arm around Rowan. "We'll see you both later."

"I'll keep you up to date as the results come in," Gordie said.

"See ya," Steve helped Doc put Malcolm's body in the special cooler.

"I'll call you later to arrange catching up, Gordie," Rowan said before they left the room.

They made their way to the back door. Quinn checked that the lock engaged when he closed it behind them. Brogan had the truck running and the heater on full blast. Quinn ushered Rowan in first and she slid across the bench seat to make room for him. The door slammed, shutting out the cold and cocooning them in a bubble of warmth.

Storm clouds darkened the day long before sunset and the small amount of snow on the ground made the drive home treacherous. Brogan took extra care as he weaved his way along the mountain road. By the time they reached the house, the wind had picked up. Leaves and branches were flying around the yard—it made the dash to the front door like a game of dodge ball. The sky opened up the second they got inside.

Rowan removed her jacket and boots but he stopped her before she could open the closet doors. They still hadn't tidied up after the last time she used it and there was no way he was opening it up tonight. He didn't have the energy to clean out the junk, all he wanted to do was crawl into bed and hold her. It had been a long day and he was more than ready for it to be over.

"We'll put our stuff by the fire to dry. I'm not risking the exploding closet again today." Quinn tugged Rowan toward the living room.

"I'll be in my office. I want to make sure William made those phone calls to the council. I'll see you two in the morning." Brogan strode down the hall and out of sight.

"Night." Rowan handed him her bundled jacket and boots. "I'm having a shower and falling into bed."

The protest on Quinn's tongue stopped when he noticed the dark circles under her eyes were back. He bent and kissed her forehead before walking into the living room to stoke the fire and lay out their gear. Rowan's sock-covered feet made no sound going up the stairs but he knew where she was by every creak of timber. Dumping the clothes on the floor by the hearth, he pulled off his boots and went to grab a couple of logs from the wood box in the corner.

It didn't take him long to get a roaring fire going and their jackets and boots spread out in front of it. He stood for a moment staring into the dancing flames, his mind on the last few days. How could so much have happen in less than a week? Pipes groaned overhead and he was reminded of the best part of the recent events. Rowan. He could picture her as she stepped into the shower. The water would stream over her shoulders and cascade down her lithe body until every naked inch of her glistened.

His cock hardened and pressed against the fly of his jeans. The denim cupped his arousal in a tight pleasure-pain grip. Damn. What was he doing downstairs fantasizing when he could be upstairs with the real thing? Quinn turned quickly, the lump on his head pounded but he ignored it. Nothing could distract him from his goal. Rowan, naked and plastered against him. Under him. Over him.

ROWAN SLID the bar of soap along her arm and coated her skin in a slippery trail of white bubbles. The wounds on the back of her hand had already begun to heal and only the largest ones stung as she cleaned away the grime left behind by the day's events. She shuddered, the danger of losing Quinn still fresh in her mind. He was safe, the danger still existed but for now they'd escaped and had a direction to go in to neutralize the threat for good.

She didn't doubt they'd find themselves a target again in the future. Marcus was involved in some way but proving it would be the challenge. Once Gordie determined the connection to the strays they would make their move. The Council would have to look at exiling him from the pack. Until they did, she would be on guard. Expect the unexpected and hope no one else got hurt in a madman's attempt to gain control.

Behind her the glass door swung open and Quinn stepped in. She looked over her shoulder to find him staring at her ass. A little wiggle produced a groan from his throat. Smiling, she tilted her hips and thrust her butt toward him. He grabbed her thighs and pulled her back. His cock pressed between her cheeks, cradled in the warm crevice. Rowan's sex clenched and grew moist with desire.

The water and soap on her body made a lubricant that allowed them to move against each other with ease. She leaned back into his embrace. His hands slid around her ribcage and up to cup her breasts. Talented fingers plucked at hardened nipples, arousing her further. Quinn nibbled along her neck, sharp bites and soft licks, he teased and tormented her. Her hips bucked, dragged his erection across sensitive flesh burning with the need to be taken.

"Can't wait," he growled in her ear.

He sucked her earlobe into his mouth, he swirled his tongue and nipped with his teeth. Hands dug into her hips, held her still as he pulled back and drove forward. She arched her back, pushed her pussy higher as the need to feel him imbedded to the hilt sliced into her. The head of his cock probed her opening and her muscles squeezed, tried to pull him in deeper. He rocked slightly, teasing them both with the promise of what was to come.

Urgency filled her. With a frustrated growl, Rowan thrust backward. His length breached her pussy and plunged deep. Stretched around hard flesh, her muscles convulsed, gripping him tight. Quinn's hand skimmed along her hipbone and zeroed in on the bundle of nerves vibrating at the top of her slit. One finger circled her clit before dipping into the cream flowing from her channel. Slick with moisture, he brought the digit back to stroke the bud protruding from its hood.

He withdrew from her heat only to plow back in at the same moment he pressed on her clit. Lightning struck. Rowan's orgasm burst out in white-hot pleasure. Her body vibrated as every nerve was lit with pure ecstasy. Quinn drove in and out of her quivering core. With blinding speed, he took her up and over another peak, shattering the last of her control. She bucked against him, his hold the only thing keeping her from collapsing to the ground.

Quinn held her in place, taking what he needed. Time after time, he rammed into her. Their legs slapped together as he continued to ride her. With her hands braced on the wall, she pushed back and tightened her muscles around his cock. He surged forward. Buried to the hilt, he flexed his pelvis and came.

Panting for breath, Rowan wobbled on her feet. Quinn slipped from her body and she slid to the floor at his feet, all energy gone. He turned off the water and opened the shower door. Large hands wrapped around her arms and pulled her up. The towel he wrapped her in was warm and soft and she snuggled into it as he dried her. Tender care and a loving touch had been missing for so long, to experience them again with Quinn was a dream come true.

Emotion swelled. Tears stung her eyes and clogged her throat. Deep breaths couldn't stop the tide. Droplets leaked to slide down her cheeks. Sniffling, she buried her face in the terrycloth to hide them from Quinn.

"Hey, are you okay? Did I hurt you?" He raised her face to his.

She smiled through watery eyes. "No. It's just so good to finally be home."

EPILOGUE

"SO YOU'RE TELLING us there's no way to prove Marcus was involved in anything that his father did?" Brogan's voice rang with frustration.

"I can prove without doubt that Malcolm Connelly turned the strays we've found in recent weeks. I can't give you anything on Marcus," Gordie's words sounded like an apology.

"Damn."

"And we have no evidence that he was involved in the cutting of Quinn's brake cable either." Rowan's heart sank. "With what we've learned about Malcolm it would be reasonable to assume he was responsible for that too."

Growls emanated from all three men in the room. Steve and Gordie had arrived ten minutes ago with news none of them wanted to hear. The council would be happy to pin all on the senior Connelly, and they'd be right to do so. It pissed her off to know Marcus would get away with what he'd done. She knew he'd been involved.

"So now what?" Steve asked.

"We watch him. He's bound to lay low for a while but we

need to keep our eyes and ears open." Brogan stood. "I'll go ring William and let him know what you found, Doc."

Quiet descended after Brogan left. No one wanted to see Marcus get off scot-free but for now their hands were tied.

"Don't worry. He's bound to slip up sooner or later and when he does we'll be there to catch him," Quinn vowed.

Need slammed into Brogan Wilder like a two-by-four to the gut. He knew lust, dealt with it when it rose, but this...

This was unlike anything he'd ever experienced. The beast inside chafed at the chains of restraint, snarled and snapped to be let free.

Brogan searched the room but nothing he could see should have him ready to shift. His sister Rowan sat on the sofa, his best friend and her fiancé, Quinn, beside her. They were the only others in the room. The fine hairs on the back of his neck stood at attention and the blood in his veins heated and pumped harder. Whatever had his instincts screaming to take, to possess, had moved closer.

Skin grew tight and hot as he fought with his inner beast. Shifting wasn't an option. Not yet. First he needed all his human skills to determine what had the power to do this to him. Then he'd have to decide if it was friend or foe. He sniffed the air, tried to place the feminine scent teasing his senses. It wasn't Rowan or any other female he knew.

"For pity's sake, Brogan, sit down. You're making *me* nervous and I know you're all bark and no bite. If you don't relax you'll scare El right back to Australia." Rowan's words broke into his agitated thoughts.

"What?" He tried to focus on his sister and what she was saying.

"Eloise. Remember? She'll be coming down from her room any minute and I want you to be on your best behavior. It took months of nagging and pleading to get her to agree to come out for the wedding. I want her to enjoy herself and not regret saying yes."

Rowan pushed off the lounge and came to stand beside him. Placing her hand on his arm she said, "Please, Brogan. She's the best friend I've had since Gordie, the only friend. She likes *me*. Not Brogan's sister."

Brogan looked at her. She was all grown up, ready to face her destiny but not without scars. They all had them but Rowan would have more if it wasn't for Eloise Crawford. He knew their friendship had been what kept his sister from going mad the few years she'd been forced to live away from home. He sucked in a deep breath and let it out slowly.

"Okay, I'll try. But something's got the beast's hackles up and I can't figure out what." He'd never hidden any of the ugly side of who or what he was from Rowan and he wouldn't do it now.

"Rowan?"

A musical voice with a strange sultry accent came at the instant his beast went on red alert and yanked at Brogan's control.

He couldn't keep the growl inside, or stop the change in his eyes that Rowan wouldn't miss. If Brogan's instincts were right, his mate had just stepped into the room.

Rowan's eyes went wide and her face drained of color. Shaking her head, she whispered, "No. Brogan, no."

Brogan squeezed his eyes shut, dragged the beast back under control. It wouldn't do to scare Eloise before they'd even met. When he opened his eyes again it was to find Rowan watching him warily. A rush of breath left her when she saw he had command of his coyote.

"It's not my choice, Rowan. The fates have spoken." He

tried to ease her with a hug. Drawing her close he murmured, "You'll need to help guide her."

"No."

"Yes, Rowan. Remember, what's done is done, we move on from here."

She pulled from his arms and stood with hands on hips. "You hurt her and I'll tear you to pieces," she snarled.

Brogan smiled. He had no doubt she'd follow through on her threat. He'd seen her go to battle for someone she cared about. Her loyalty to those she loved was unquestionable, but if those she loved were pitted against each other she always sided with the weaker one.

Rowan looked past him to the woman who stood twenty feet away and had his body reacting as if she were plastered to his side. He could smell her, almost taste her. If he didn't get a hold of himself he had no doubt Eloise Crawford would run screaming into the hills or to the nearest airport and first plane out of there.

"El, you've unpacked?" Rowan asked as she stepped around him.

Brogan looked at Quinn, who'd remained suspiciously quiet during the little demo of his animal behavior. Their gazes connected and he could see the laughter in his best friend's eyes. The bastard knew this wouldn't be easy and if Quinn knew anything about him, he knew everything. As he knew Quinn. He wouldn't fool himself into thinking Quinn felt sorry for him. Oh, no. To Brogan's way of thinking, Quinn was looking forward to the inevitable fight to come.

http://www.rhiancahill.com/books/coyote-hunger/coyote-wild/

ABOUT THE AUTHOR

Rhian Cahill is the alter ego of a former stay-at-home mother of four. With motherly duties rapidly dwindling Rhian is able to make use of the fertile imagination she used to keep herself sane for all those years of slavery. Having spent years living overseas and visiting tropical climates has helped inspire some steamy stories.

Multi-published in erotic romance and contemporary romance, Rhian, with the help of Mr. Muse, spends her days and nights writing.

When not glued to the keyboard you'll find her book or knitting in hand avoiding any and all housework as much as possible.

For more on Rhian –

Website – http://www.rhiancahill.com/
Newsletter signup – http://www.rhiancahill.com/contact/newsletter/
Twitter – https://twitter.com/RhianCahill
FaceBook – https://www.facebook.com/RhianCahillAuthor
Instagram – http://instagram.com/rhiancahill/
BookBub – https://www.bookbub.com/authors/rhian-cahill
Goodreads page - https://www.goodreads.com/rhian_cahill

LOOK FOR THESE TITLES BY RHIAN CAHILL

Coyote Hunger Series

Coyote Home – Book 1

Coyote Wild – Book 2

Coyote Whispers – Book 3

Coyote Lies – Book 4

Coyote Law – Book 5

Party Games Series

Truth Or Dare

Spin The Bottle

Pass The Parcel – Novella

Are You Game Series

7 Minutes In Heaven – Book 1

Catch'n'Kiss – Book 2

Red Light, Green Light – Book 3

Hearts Are Wild Series

No More Talking (novella)

Dare You To (novella)

Mad Love

For a full list of Rhian's available books visit her website

http://www.rhiancahill.com/books/